Repeat This and You're Dead

Repeat This
and You're Dead

Lawrence Russell

Porcépic Books
an imprint of
Beach Holme Publishers
Victoria, B.C.

This edition is published by Beach Holme Publishers, 4252 Commerce Circle, Victoria, B.C., V8Z 4M2 with the assistance of The Canada Council and the B.C. Ministry of Small Business, Tourism and Culture. This is a Porcépic Book.

Printed and bound in Canada by Webcom.

Front Cover Design, Photography: Rick McGrath
Editor: Dave Godfrey

Canadian Cataloguing in Publication Data

Russell, Lawrence, 1942-
        Repeat this and you're dead

"A Porcépic Book."
ISBN 0-88878-363-9

        I. Title.
PS8585.U77R46 1995   C813'.54   C95-910069-5
PR9199.3.R87R46 1995

To Ballantine

Contents

The Bomb

WHEN YOU LOOK at Ireland today, what with all its killings and unemployment, and compare it to what it was like when I was just a cub who couldn't keep his nose clean, it's enough to make you weep. You take the Knockan Bridge, for example, where they recently found that girl half-dead because some bastard shot her through the knees. That used to be a great old place. Me and my pals used to go there in the evenings to smoke a fag, shoot the breeze, sit on the wall, watch the girls, arm-wrestle, penny pitch, have a good old time. That's where the travelling fairs used to set up, down on the river bank. Lots of grass for the ponies, space for the tents and amusement machines. It was all good fun then. They got in trouble once, though, because one of the gypsies that ran the Hell Wheel went after a local girl, raped her, people in the village said, but that blew over and it was mostly just good fun.

The funniest night was the one when we thought we'd put a bomb on the bridge, just for the hell of it, because someone had tried to blow up a telephone box down in Enniskillen near the Border, and wasn't that a pitiful exercise? The IRA called it a "blow for freedom". I made the bomb, as it was my idea and I had the parts, and it was good enough to fool that idiot Sloan, the long string of pump water that he was, and send him hell for leather on his bike to get the Sergeant, and it was good enough to fool him too, make him send for the Army. Me and my mates decided it was time to leave the bushes, take a long walk, put some distance between ourselves and the Knockan Bridge. We spent a couple of hours in town, hanging around Joe's Cafe, throwing peas at the girls, and I remember Duck spat in his coffee, so's none of us would drink it when he was in the Gents. Ah, it was good fun then. Those were the days.

When we got back to the village, all hell had broken loose, the B-Specials had a road block up and the Army were out in the fields, combing the ditches and woods. I saw Sloan standing beside an armoured car, said to him, what's up? Sloan said, there's a bomb on the bridge, I found it. No fooling, said Duck. It was all I could do to not laugh in his face, but you know, this thing had got way out of hand, way way out of hand, and even though I hated Sloan there wasn't any way I could tell him he was an idiot. The Bomb Man wasn't fooled. He could see it was just an old radio chassis in a shoe box. He started laughing, tossed it to the Sergeant, who didn't laugh at all. The Sergeant walked back to the village with the box in his arms and a hard look on his old face, ignored all the people, went straight into the barracks.

Oh they interrogated Sloan for a long time over this one but people said it was the IRA for sure, a big black car had driven onto the bridge and a woman had put the box beside the wall before speeding off with three hard men. Some people knew it had been a hoax but most believed it was the real thing. In the end they blamed the gypsies and sent them packing and there were no more fairs at the Knockan Bridge. We had some good laughs, me and my mates, but it was a terrible secret to carry, terrible.

Things are different now, though. You heard about the bomb in that church in Enniskillen? It killed twenty-seven people, most of them women and children. It was terrible, just terrible. Aye, it's a lot different now. Back then, you see, we were just pretending.

Rathlin Island

I FIRST SAW RATHLIN ISLAND when I was at the Lamass Fair in Ballycastle but at that time I didn't know it was the place Marconi made his first radio transmissions from, although I did know Robert the Bruce hid out there in a cave and saw the spider which gave him the inspiration to hang tough against the English. I could see it was bleak, with no trees and little sign of life, and nothing to recommend it, so it was easy to go back to eating my candy floss and watch the man on the grass try to escape from the straight-jacket he'd donned for the amusement of the crowd.

Not long after that my Uncle said he was going to Rathlin to buy some sheep, and I had to go because I was learning the business. It took us an hour and a bit to get there from the quay in Ballycastle in an open boat which was powered by a single stroke engine and steered by an Islander called Black Bob. It was overcast and I remember how the clouds seemed to merge with the heaving slate mass of the ocean, so that the Island disappeared altogether at times. My Uncle and I had sweaters on below our jackets but we weren't really dressed properly for this kind of gallivant. Both of us were extremely happy when we came into the bay which was sheltered from the North Atlantic wind and when Black Bob cut the motor back and we glided with a soft hiss over the smooth water, we were happier still.

He pointed over the side. We could see a large dark shape

perhaps thirty fathoms below and although it was dilating because of the swell, it was easy to see that it was a large sunken wreck. A German battle cruiser, said Black Bob. She came in here on fire in 1916 and went down taking most of the crew.... Most of the crew. A shiver went up the back of my neck. There was something unreal and fantastic about it and as the phantom shape receded and we headed for the beach, I could imagine the sailors, their uniforms on fire, jumping blindly into the night....

As they loaded the sheep into the boat, all forty of them, I hunted for sticks of cordite among the shells and in the sand. There was plenty of it, and it still burned when I put a match to it. So I sat there, igniting stick after stick of this flotsam from the wreck, as the shepherds and their dogs kept the sheep tight on the beach. That's what I remember about Rathlin Island: cordite. I don't remember anything about the buildings, radio masts or caves in the cliffs... just cordite.

Black Bob wanted to return to the mainland right away because it looked as though the weather might get ugly and it did, the wind coming up as soon as we cleared the bay. It was something to be jammed in amongst all those bleating sheep as the boat laboured up and down those waves and my Uncle's face went red from the wind and the spray, and it was certainly something when we realized we weren't going to make it, as the tide was pulling us to the North and the open sea. There were moments when I couldn't even hear the engine on its stroke and as we started to get swamped, my Uncle shouted at Black Bob who was standing stoically at the tiller. My Uncle started shouting at me and I couldn't understand a word he was saying but when he grabbed a ewe and heaved it overboard, I knew what I had to do.

They must've been cheap, those sheep, because I don't know why anybody would want to go to Rathlin Island in an open boat. I certainly learned something about business that day, and a lot more about fear. Some people join fairs and escape from straight-jackets to make their money, while others take a trip to an island and just throw it away.

Cargo Cult

JAMES' OBSESSION WITH AIRPLANES is easily under-
standable: his father was a test pilot in the RAF during the
Second World War and one of his earliest memories is of
the wrecked Lancasters and Spitfires littering the fields
around the aerodrome where his father was based. His parents separated at the end of the War and he was sent to
live with his relatives on an old estate in Ulster. He thought
it was temporary. He thought he was only going to be there
two or three weeks. It was a holiday, and soon he would
be back with his parents.

It wasn't so, and in fact James never saw his father again,
even though he continued to dream of him. He could see
him in his uniform, see him climbing into a fighter plane,
see him sliding the cockpit shut, see him giving the "thumbs
up", see him taxi onto the runway and take off, see him
spiralling up into the clouds like the lark.... There was a con-
spiracy of silence, you see. For a long time he believed what
they told him, that his father would be over to see him, might
even fly there, and so James would wander the estate, looking in the fields for the aircraft, and indeed there were any
number of level areas where an aircraft could land.

Gradually James began to sense something wasn't right
but before cynicism and its deadly instinct for the truth got
the hold of him, one summer an uncle came to the estate

for a short holiday. This uncle perhaps felt sorry for him and, thinking it would be creative and educational, introduced him to the hobby of model airplanes. In the evenings they laboured over the construction of a large balsa model which, the uncle guaranteed, would definitely fly. But just before the model was completed, James accidentally stepped on the frame, crushing it, and the uncle just threw up his hands and retired to the sitting room for a glass of Bushmills. James was heartbroken and struggled to reconstruct the ruined frame, but although he made a valiant effort, the model was never good enough to fly.

Anyway, this started James building models, and over the years he made hundreds, some of them beautiful to look at, but all with the same characteristic: there was some flaw that made them incapable of flight. It was obvious to his relatives that he wasn't all there, there was something slightly wrong with him. He wasn't violent or dangerous, and he would work if he was told, but the problem was, the work he did as often as not turned out to be useless. Take the big field down by the cattle pond, for example: he was supposed to have ploughed that for potatoes but instead he tried to level a track a couple of hundred yards long and twenty wide and when they asked him what the hell he thought he was doing, he just cut the engine of the bulldozer and sat at one end waiting. That was five years ago and you can still see the mark of it and you can still see James hanging around down there, watching the sky. It was a runway, of course, although the poor bastard knew his father was dead, had been for years, and would never be coming back to Ireland.

That's what you call a "cargo cult" — when you try to imitate the machines of the Gods you once knew in order to try and lure them back. The locals think of James as being mad, but is it madness to want to be reconciled with your parent? If so, then all human endeavour is vanity and madness. We must be fair. You see, I know James extremely well: he could've been me.

The Weeping Eye
of the Chipped Virgin

I KNEW MARY O'NEIL because I went to the Tech with her, and although she was a Catholic, I couldn't resist her. Laugh. Go ahead. It wasn't so long ago that they lined them all up on one side of the yard and us on the other, and they went inside with the priest and we went inside with the minister. Religious Instruction was compulsory in those days, but I must admit it failed completely with me.

Jesus, Mary was a sexy little thing, mature beyond her years, looked twenty when we had our romance. She lived miles away towards the Bann River, right on the edge of Republican country, so we used to meet on a Friday or Saturday night in Belfast where no one would know us. We'd take in a flick at the Opera House or go to Kelly's Cellars, that pub where you could sit on barrels, but mostly we went into a dark alley and made love. Mary was the first for me. She said I was the first for her but you know, thinking about it now, that doesn't seem likely.

She was the one who got pregnant by some married bloke and somehow managed to conceal the fact from her family, until she went into the yard of the Chapel at Longcross and lay down in front of the statue of the Virgin and went into labour, and damnit, didn't she die there by herself giving birth. You might've read about that. You certainly read about what happened a couple of years later when her younger sister, girl of fourteen or fifteen, tried to commit suicide on the same spot by taking a dose of pills and said she was saved from death because the one good eye of the Virgin shed a tear. Fantastic, isn't it, how they can believe an old piece of chipped stone like that could come alive and shed tears for Mary O'Neil and her sister and then the priests go and make a bloody shrine out of the place and all sorts of people come traipsing there to donate money and get healed for what ails them. A miracle, they called it. I suppose this shows why they're different from us: they can make a profit out of illusion, while we can only make it from sweat.

She broke it off, not me. I think some priest was onto her. I often think of what might've happened if I'd been the father of Mary's child... indeed, I feel as if maybe I was, and I don't know why because I never loved her, although I loved loving her and she loving me, licking my tears in the darkness.

Bad Milk

I'VE JUST COME FROM THE FUNERAL of that rich uncle of mine, the one who was a member of the Orange Lodge and slept with a pistol below his pillow, and I flew a hellofa long way for it too. I don't know why I bothered. Last time I visited he looked at my rattan shoes and tropical suit and said, normally we shoot fellas like you. If he hadn't paid for the bloody meal, I would've just left and gone to the pub with the canary that I always visit when I'm here.

You might know him, you might not. He owned that big dairy, made a fortune selling milk to school children, and if you went to school here, chances are you drank his milk. One time I used to admire him and why not? He drove a Lagonda coupe, had lots of money in his pocket and a nice looking secretary trailing after him. The last one, the one he married, I knew because she was in my class in school, for Chrissake. That was bad. I even had a roll with her myself first time I came back for a visit and went to the dairy looking for him. Later, I found out he thought she was *his* property. To think he dumped my Aunt Deirdre for her, Aunt D. with her sweet Donegal accent and lovely black eyes, the mother of his two children, and them big enough to be married themselves. She just went completely alcoholic and died in poverty, and I regret missing her funeral, but I never knew a thing about it, because I was on the other side of the world.

Oh he was a pillar of society around here, and I can't think why he didn't get himself elected to Stormount. But then, they went into Direct Rule from Westminster, didn't they? He participated in that book burning they had, told me himself, chucked *The Naked Lunch* into the fire, and a bunch of other titles he decided were obscene or had Fenian overtones. You should see his bloody house. *That's* obscene. His grand masters' paintings and silverware, the statue of King Billy on his horse Stor, that loyalist artifact he thinks is worth so much money, worth more than his trout stream and his horses, worth more than his young wife. I mean, who knows who King Billy is outside of the six counties? All Billy was was a Dutchman who lucked out when the English Protestants asked him to come over and get rid of their Catholic King. William of Orange. The heir of Cromwell. It's all a bore.

The Orangeman. My Uncle, and thank God he's not the only uncle. When he got drunk, he'd put on his orange sash and white gloves and bowler hat and stagger around the house singing loyalist songs, scare the maid, scare the dog, but he didn't scare anyone that really knew him, like his ninety-two-year old mother whom he neglected entirely, left her to fend for herself in the house where he was born. Think about that. His own mother.

Well he's dead now, heart got him says Eileen, but who knows? Maybe he ate a piece of poisoned potato bread. If you'd seen those men at the grave, with their wool suits, orange sashes, and bowler hats, and those UDA fellas in their flak jackets and automatics, you might think there was something unnatural about it. He had enemies, and they weren't all Republicans either. He did a lot of shouting about the Pope, but he never did business with the Pope, so I'm sure it was one of his own that got him. He killed a child once, years ago when he was drunk, ran over him on a country road when he was driving like Juan Fangio, the only Catholic I ever heard him admire. He used his money and his Lodge connections to get out of that one and he did the same over the Bad Milk Scandal. Of course he was a Mason too and you know what they're like, a nod, a wink, the secret sign and you rule the goddamn world. Everywhere you go it's the same: good business is bad business and by that, I mean *dirty*.

Why am I so moral? So ungrateful? So disloyal? It's got nothing to do with whether or not he's left me anything in his will. Not at all. Because, why would he? He had closer family, and anyway, he left his wife and I can catch my plane any time.

Alias Boswell and Johnson

DID YOU KNOW THAT RASCAL James Boswell, the man who wrote the biography of Dr. Johnson and who molested a woman at a funeral, actually visited Belfast once? He did. He had relatives there, a cousin called Annie and I think he tried her too, but let me tell you, if he went there today, he'd find things to be vastly different. I did. For one, there's a bloody big army helicopter hanging over the Falls Road area day and night, and you can see it from miles away, even when you're coming into the city on that motorway from Antrim.

My guide, whom I'll call Johnson, was a veterinarian who hadn't been out of the house on a tear for years, and used the opportunity of my visit to get loose in the city. So we start out in a dive called Dubarry's, a pub I vaguely remember from our university days. There are a few old gaffers in one corner listening to a dog race on the radio, and none of the other patrons look anything like us, especially me. When we're finishing our first round a fellow comes in and stands at the bar beside Johnson, and soon the both of them get to talking. Johnson buys him a Bushmills, says, do you know where a man can have a good sexual time? This fellow looks him over, looks me over, says, where're you from? Ballymena, says Johnson, and the fellow nods slowly before smiling and saying, ah, well you'll be alright in here, boys, nobody'll give you any trouble. He motions to this woman who's sitting against the wall with her legs crossed, digging around in her purse looking for a match for her unlit fag, and she gets up, totters over, pulls herself onto a stool between Johnson and this fellow with the small moustache and thick glasses, orders a gin and tonic as our pimp says, this is Angela, what's yer names? Johnson, says my veterinarian friend. Boswell, I say. He looks at me, says, Boswell? Ballymena? A long time ago, I say. He's on a visit from Canada, says my friend, I want to make sure he has a good time in Ireland. Angela is nodding, her hard face stupid with drink or something, then she goes back to her table to collect her change. My friend goes to pay for her gin and tonic but the fellow stays his hand, leans across says, let her pay for her own, you don't want her, she's a whore. A whore's fine, says Johnson, but this fellow says, nah, stay clear of her, she's trouble. When she comes back she sits on the other side of this man who has now brought out his I.D. card, which says he's a prison guard at the Maze.

Jesus, I'm thinking, this man is UDA for sure, and what's Johnson getting us into, but Johnson's unfazed, says he's got a cousin who's also a guard at the Maze. Johnson? says Maze, his eyes tightening, but my friend says the name is different, it's McColgin. I know him! says Maze. Des McColgin, right? And everything's fine and dandy in Dubarry's as we knock back our lagers and whiskies and flirt with Death... because, be realistic, in these places in this city in these times, Death is never far away.

I can see Johnson's happy enough with the Pirahna (as I've come to think of her, because her mouth bulges as if she's got an extra set of braces behind those teeth) and he's now pressing his corpulent stomach against her thigh as he leans suavely against the bar pretending to listen to Maze as he rattles on about cousin Des and all the hard men in the Maze, interned without trial, the hunger strikes, the martyrs, the grasses, the screeching women outside the gates and the stress of it all but sure the money's no so bad if ye can stand the agro. Suddenly he says, drink up, boys, I'll take ye somewhere else. We down our drinks as Angela the Pirahna badgers Johnson for another fag and as he lights her,

I look at Maze, and the scar on his sunken cheek and the marbles behind those thick glasses say it all: *somewhere else.* Outside in the failing light I can still hear the heavy engine of that big helicopter in the distance, still hear it over the noise of the traffic and the machinery on the docks. Maze is driving a gold Italian sports coupe and bids us follow him in our vehicle, which Johnson seems all too eager to do. I say, why don't we cruise past Queen's, check out the Botanic for old times' sake, those university girls must look good, but Johnson seems like a man on a mission, his eyes are locked on another wavelength, and I'm thinking, well, *he* should know, *he* lives here, *he* is fluent in the ways of the Natives. But where were we going, following this gold car into the darkened recesses of the industrial area, these cobble-stone streets and Victorian warehouses? Is this in our best interests? As we engage the labyrinth, I think of what the real Dr. Johnson once said: *There is as much charity in helping a man downhill as there is in helping him uphill.* We loop the block twice and Maze pulls over, comes back to our car, says (cheerily), you'll be alright here, boys. Johnson squints through the windshield, says, looks quiet. Maze says, I had to get ye out of that place, you weren't safe there. His clip-on shades are masking those marbles now, so I can't tell if he's joking or what, and he returns to his car and disappears. We sit for awhile and nothing happens. We then circle the block slowly, doing two, three laps and I'm urging Johnson to forget it, let's go to the Botanic, when lo! a woman appears. Where did she come from, I'm thinking, how did she get here? The walls are bland, almost featureless, and the only thing I could think was that she'd dropped in from the roof. Johnson beckons her over. What a tart, he growls, his eyes glassy, his fingers opening and closing on the steering wheel in nervous anticipation. But she remains on the other side of the street, stiff in her tight skirt, stiff all over like a dummy, and when I see the masked figure on the roof suddenly illuminated in an instant of passing light, I realize that is exactly what she is: a dummy.

We were lucky to get out of that one, let me say. Lucky we never got out of the car, lucky Johnson had the instinct for escape that got us, tires screaming, out of that maze. Old Belfast isn't what it was. There are all sorts of people running around representing themselves as something they aren't, and if this means a helicopter gunship hanging over it day and night, that's fine with me.

The Letter

IT WAS A MISTAKE sending the letter to him, thinking he would pass it on to Joan, because he had designs on her himself, even though she was his cousin and a year older. Joan had a reputation of being fast, and she had good legs and good legs excited him more than a nice mouth even, although a mouth like hers came a decent second on his list of criteria. When he saw her at the dance that Saturday night he told her about the letter, but that he'd forgotten it, which was true. He didn't tell her he'd received the letter more than a month ago and could've passed it on to her at school during lunchtime when she usually took a walk up the street with one of her friends to look in the shop windows or have a coffee and sweet in Joe's.

Who is this fellow? he asked her as they danced a fox trot around the small clubhouse floor, and she laughed and said, Nobody. Well, if he was Nobody, what was he writing to her for? Why didn't he send it to her directly instead of to him, her cousin? Nobody must be a Dogan, he thought. Or it must be a dirty letter. That was it — she wouldn't want her mother reading a dirty letter from some bloke she met that summer when she had that job in Portrush working as a receptionist in a Guest House.

When they stepped outside for a breather, Duck came up on his scooter and invited her for a ride and she hopped onto the pillion and they went around the perimeter of the playing field. Later Duck asked him if he was taking her home, and he said, don't be daft, she's my cousin, and Duck said, that wouldn't stop me. Not much stopped Duck. His morals were like his teeth: stained and dirty, and his dirty smile seemed to get him what he wanted because Joan let Duck take her home that night. But next week at the dance, when it came to Ladies' Choice, she crossed the floor for him and they were dancing as always. Have you got the letter, she said to him, and he said, damnit, I forgot it. Then she accused him of having opened the letter and reading it, and when she said this, she was clearly teasing him, and he didn't know what to think of her. He wondered about Duck, and wondered if Joan was as easy as they said. He asked her if she was going home alone. She pulled back her head to look at him, and as she smiled, he noticed that she was definitely cross-eyed, although this characteristic wasn't unattractive. In fact, it made her more sexual, and he was afraid to draw his body close to her again because she would recognize his helpless arousal.

He didn't walk her home that night and the next week Duck showed up again and was bragging openly about his success with Big Joan, and while there was a chance that Duck was lying because sex was the only topic of conversation he had, there was something preventing Joan being anything more than a fantasy. Besides, there were other girls, some of them much better looking, some of them with no reputations at all, so he consoled himself with the notion that he might start one for Olive, the Dentist's Assistant, or Sadie, the Education Student, or even the prettiest of them all, Desdemona, the Dustman's Daughter....

One afternoon he opened the letter and read it, because, he reasoned, it was too old now to be of real consequence. It said: *Darling Joan, it has been so long since I last saw you that my heart aches. Last summer was the most deliriously happy time in my life. Please don't think me mad, because when I say I love you, I mean it. Remember our times together, dancing at the Arcadia? Or our walks on the Esplanade? I can't believe that we must go our separate ways as you said the last time. Darling, my heart just aches, and I can't stand it. I tried once to phone you but some man answered, your father I expect, or perhaps it was the wrong number. I won't do that again. I'm back at school, but it looks no good, I can't do it. All I want is to tell you I love you and it will be forever. I take this opportunity to return your photo. Please write....*

When he looked at the photo, it shocked him: it was Joan alright and she was naked, reclining in the sand like one of those post cards of Bridget Bardot, only this was Joan and she looked obscene. His arousal was immediate and fantastic, yet at the same time he hated her. It was inexplicable, this jealousy, because she had never made him suffer, or had she ever refused him the opportunity to try and suffer. Nobody was suffering, and wasn't he lucky, because that was the greatest experience a woman could allow a man.

He took a pen, and a piece of paper, and copied out the letter, but instead of mentioning the photograph, he wrote: *Don't feel you need to write. By the time you get this, I will be dead. Yours always, Nobody.* A few days later he passed the letter to one of her friends, but much to his surprise and total chagrin, she made no attempt to contact him for an explanation. He didn't see her at the dance the next week or the one after, and it was a month or more before he ran into her on the street. She just smiled, said she was going to the Tech in Belfast now, said she was doing some shopping for her mother, said she had to go. It wasn't her legs he saw this time, or her mouth, or the long white body in the dunes, but her travelling eyes, which were looking right past him.

Now he knew what it was like to be Nobody.

The Tomb

THERE ALWAYS COMES A TIME when you do something you've been told not to, whether it's because you've
a natural disrespect for the law like most of the Irish, or
because you're just plain ignorant. When I decided to follow the tunnel that channelled the water from the dam
behind the house to the big meadow at the front was just
such a time. I was twelve or thirteen and had already sur-
vived a couple of injuries which deluded me into thinking
I could survive anything, that life never stopped, that it just
flowed like the stream I followed that day.

I was under the sway of Hearkness, one of our occasional
labourers, and easily goaded by his bravado and duped by
his stories. He was the one who told me about the cellars
and the tomb they contained, about the body of Sir James,
the gentleman who built the house sometime after the Plantation of Ulster, who lay there in a stone coffin to keep his
ghost from wandering the estate but that the lid had been
left unsealed, so that he wandered anyway.... For a year I
lost a lot of sleep thinking about that tomb. A lot. Some
nights my bed would drop through the floors all the way
to cellars; others, Sir James would rise through the walls and
enter my room and stand at the end of my bed where I lay
frozen, eyes swollen and incomprehending, a window of
darkness between us.

But I also knew Hearkness was a liar, because he'd never paid me for the shotgun cartridges I'd stolen from my Uncle on his suggestion. And I knew I'd never be free from his dominion until I exposed his assertions for what they were: false insinuations and cunning lies.

You couldn't enter the cellars any more from the house, because the entrance was mortared over and sealed off by a set of cupboards in the scullery. So the only way into them was to follow the underground stream and this is what I did one bright and sunny day when the cattle were grazing easily in the meadow, free from paranoia and uneasy dreams. I entered the tunnel, crouched over and wading against the flow, my flashlight illuminating the stone masonry and the shallow, fast water ahead. The stream was used to drive a turbine which powered a corn crusher at one time, but more recently a small saw mill. The turbine was at the bottom of a twenty foot shaft which gated into the tunnel at the back of the house, so you could see there had to be some truth to the notion that the stream passed through the cellars, and might've been the place where the women did the washing in the old days.

The fear of encountering Sir James or rats wasn't as great as the fear of suffocation, the idea that the roof might collapse and I'd be buried alive in this ancient culvert, but I pressed on because I had confidence in my new flashlight, as it was the same one Hearkness strapped to the barrel of his shotgun to shoot owls with, and he never missed. When I stopped to get my breath, I could hear the forlorn sound the stream now made, a fluting sound, the sort of sound you get when you blow on a pop bottle. I thought, that's the shaft where the turbine rests, I must be getting close....

I don't know how far I waded up that stream, but at the time, it seemed like a mile. But when the water grew deeper, almost filling my rubber boots, there I was, I was in the cellar, the beam from my flashlight drifting slowly over the fronds of spider webbing which stretched like dead skin between the arches or hung in silent veils from the buttresses. The stone walls glistened with sweat and the elegant patterns of slugs. Yet there was no coffin or sarcophagus that I could see — only what appeared to be the remains of some wine barrels and bits of lathing. I was standing in a small canal which cut through one side of the cellar floor and which obviously led to the turbine. Just as I was trying to climb out, my flashlight rolled from the floor and dropped into the water and went out as it sank. My God in heaven! Fear spasmed through me as the dead light of the centuries buried me where I hung, half out of the canal. I slipped back slowly and stood there as the water rushed against my boots like an endless horde of yelping rats and the draft made the stilled turbine moan in the cold echo of the sealed cellar.

There was a tomb there, alright, and it took this special darkness to see it. It was my own tomb, if I stayed here in this place, in this house, in this country, with its stone coffins and underground streams. And what was the future if all I could become was yet another Irish ghost like Sir James or a liar like Hearkness? I knew one day I would leave this place, even if I had to pass through walls to do it.

The Hand

YOU'RE LOOKING AT ME now in disbelief, not accepting what you're hearing. But it's true, and I'll prove it to you. They cut off his hand, honest to God, as sure as I'm lying in this bed with these tubes coming out of my arms, Mrs. Black. You know yourself what a pack of bad rascals are abroad in the streets of Belfast these days, sure the papers are full of it, it's just desperate what's going on. You can see my head's full of gray hairs, and you know, I'm not even thirty-nine years old. It's this business with Michael that's put me in here, no doubt about it, as my heart was fine after the last operation.

He fell in with a bad crowd, all because of a girl he took up with. Protestants, and I'm sure you won't take offence, Mrs. Black, when I tell you that, because there's bad ones on both sides. Her brother was the ringleader, the one that got Michael to rob Shelly's discotheque, and he was the only one that got caught, and sure he was lucky enough to get off with probation, but he was stupid enough to stick with that girl. He put her in a family way, you see, and she wouldn't marry him as he was Catholic, her brother was adamant about that, and I don't suppose we thought much of it either, for, honestly, does it ever work? I'm lying here in my bed just across from you in yours and we're just two human beings in the hands of God, regardless of our religion. But it's this society that divides us, not our hearts, or who was here first, or who really owns this land.

They were drinking, her brother and his gang, and gang's the word I use because that's what they are, for I know they've done some very bad things, and this thing they did to my son was one of them. They were drunk and they said to him, if you're really with us, Mike, if you're really an Ulsterman and not a Fenian bastard, you can prove it. And he said, how can I prove it any more than I already have, boys? I love Rita but you won't let me marry her, and sure didn't I take the rap for the Shelly's job, what else can I do? They said to him, you can give us your right hand, Mike, go on, here's a knife, and when Michael wouldn't do it, they set on him, God help him, and they cut his hand off. Right off, and then they left him there, and if it hadn't been for Rita, he would've bled to death right where it happened in the kitchen, Mrs. Black.

You're still not believing it, are you. Surely it could've been stitched back on, you're thinking. Oh they tried, they tried right here in this hospital, right here in the Royal, but it wouldn't take again, and now he's fit for nothing, can't work, just follows this Rita around like a dog, even though she's taken up with another man, had the baby adopted. What time does the clock on the wall say? It's almost visiting hours, isn't it? He'll be here shortly, my Michael, he's very loyal, never misses a visit when I'm in. I'll get him to show you, Mrs. Black, and you can see for yourself. I said I could prove it and I will.

Transatlantic Call

TONY MY MAN, IT'S ME... yeah, really. I've got a bottle of Bushmills here I'm working my way through, was thinking about you, about the old days, thought I'd give you a call, see if you were still alive or what. Did you get my card from Mexico? Well I'm not in Mexico now, but close. Five star hotel, white sand beach, bluest water you've ever seen, cheap booze, Jesus, they had Bushmills in the Duty Free, so here I am. What's it doing in Bogland — raining? Sure it's raining, what else does it ever do. But Tony, I didn't call to talk about the weather, no. The last time I saw you, when was that? Five years ago, anyway. When I was over for my uncle's funeral, you said I'd been a member of the Orange Lodge, and I denied it. Well I remember the circumstances now and I admit it: I joined the Orange Lodge.

You're laughing. I'm glad to hear it, because the last time you looked haggard, something about late calls to lonely farms to remove bullets from fellas that couldn't go to the hospital. You don't remember. Exactly. Like me and the Orange Lodge. Well my friend you joined it too. It was when we got tossed out of the Scouts, and you said let's join the Orangemen and learn to play the flute. That's right, the flute. I only lasted a week, and turned the bloody thing back in, never got a sash or anything, but what about you, my friend, when did you quit? The same time? Bullshit. I think you're still in there.

Of course I'm drunk, what about you? Can't drink? What, the ulcer? Oh it's seven o'clock in the morning there. Too bad. The party's just starting here. Can you hear that tropical music? *Hey hey caramba!* You should be here, Tony, we could have some times. You and me, we were terrors. Remember why we were thrown out of the Scouts? I do. We tortured Nipper and tied him up and hung him from the coat rack and because it was a weekend, they didn't find him for three days. Nipper, what a bloody weasel, he was jealous because we were Patrol Leaders and he squealed about us keeping the money we falsely solicited by saying it was for a Jamboree. You remember that, don't you? Sure, it's been a long time. Thirty years ago, more. It's like a dream to me, Tony, like a dream. What, Nipper's a policeman now? In Rhodesia. Hey, that's Zimbabwe, man. Get in the twentieth century.

Sure the call is costing an arm and leg, but what's money? It feels good to talk to you, to confess, to get that business about the Lodge out of my head. They're psychopaths, man. It's all ritual without any culture. At least the Fenians have a few good writers, don't you think... you don't read, haven't got the time. Do I hear a fry going in the background? Have you got the pan on the stove, got the eggs and rashers blazing away, a slab of soda bread in there maybe? No no, not me. It's all croissants and coffee now.

Where do I live now? Don't know, actually. Head office is still in California, but they might send me anywhere. Right now I don't care, I got this whiskey, stuff I never usually drink, but I'm drinking it now, 'cause I was just thinking about you and that stuff about the Orange Lodge. Funny thing, when I get drunk, I start to talk Irish, but when I'm sober, I'm just another North American. You can hear that, can't you? It's still in me, like a lost fart, eh. Well, I'll let you go, old pal, let you put on that stethoscope so you can start checking those heifer's hearts, those pigs, those sheep, those bloody Orangemen with their accidental bullet wounds.

You're still laughing. Good. *Adios amigo.* And listen: don't kid me, I think you're still in there.

Repeat This and You're Dead

IT WAS A LONG WAY to the St. Peter place from his Uncle's farm, so he chose to go through the fields, follow the river where he used to gindle for trout in the shallows or swim in the pools a few years ago when he was young enough to get out of working in the summers. It was a pleasant walk, made all the more so by the knowledge that the tractor he'd accidentally set on fire had been repaired and the insurance would pay for it. His Uncle had been quite understanding, even though the accident had been entirely his fault and unnecessary. He'd tried to pour the vaporizing oil into the tank without shutting off the engine and when some of the fuel was spilled, the tractor burst into flames. He'd been lucky, actually — all he got was a few singed hairs on one side of his head and wrist and a bad scare.

The St. Peter place was close to the village and the river led right to it. Riley St. Peter no longer farmed; instead he did agricultural equipment repairs in one of the old stone outbuildings behind the house. People made jokes about Riley — they said he let the pigs and hens wander through the house, that he was a "homo", that he was mad, that he was living under an alias, all sorts of things that James knew were ridiculous. Riley was odd-looking right enough. He reminded James of *The Hunchback of Notredam* because of his heavy lips and slouching walk.

He came into the yard past the midden where a few fowl

and pigs were resting in the sun. He wondered if the dog would come after him but all was silent as he made his way towards the garage. There was a new Mini parked in the yard and he wondered who had come to see Riley. But just as he came up to the arched doorway, he stopped: Riley and his visitor were having a heated argument about something.

James lingered beside a derelict sward-turner, intimidated, uncertain as to what to do. *It's a lie,* he heard Riley snarl, *none of your bloody business anyway.* The other man laughed, said something about "his readers". His accent was English, maybe London. There was a clink as a heavy wrench or crowbar struck metal in a grating oscillation, and the man backed out of the garage with Riley after him. The man was young, dressed in a jacket and tie, and as he waved his notebook, he said, *I think you owe us an explanation, Peters... why would an Englishman change his name to assume an Irish identity and involve himself in paramilitary politics? That's what we want to know, that's what we have a right to know.* Riley, hunched in his oily overalls, stopped, his body heaving with rage as he faced his arrogant visitor. Neither had yet noticed James, who simply wanted to slink away, pretend this had never happened, but if he moved, they would see him. The man was nodding at Riley in the all-knowing fashion, but when Riley sprang towards him, he turned and ran for his car. Riley scurried back into the garage, then reappeared with a tire-iron which he threw at the car as the man backed it hastily out of the yard, scattering the animals. As James started to edge away he could see his Uncle's tractor sitting in the garage where Riley had obviously been working on it, but this was irrelevant now.

Riley muttered *bloody sodding bastard* in clear English tones but as he turned and saw James running towards the river he was all Irish when he shouted, *repeat this and you're dead!*

The Wild Colonial Boy

WE CALLED THEM FITS when I was a kid in Ireland and the person I knew who had them was a fellow by the name of Hearkness, Billy Hearkness. He was three or four years older than me and the one who introduced me to masturbation and the killing of animals for pleasure. He had a gun and a ferret and he'd hunt for rabbits mostly but he wasn't adverse to shooting a seagull or a small robin for the hell of it. Any creature, great or small, was a legitimate target for practice. I even seen him snipe Mr. McAllister one day when he was in the field inspecting his cattle, a couple of rounds close to his ear which went ricochetting off the stone dyke and sent the old boy diving for cover. Hearkness was what you'd call "a bad egg".

He had black oily hair and thick lips and if he'd had an earring he would've passed for a gypsy, one of those fellas who run the amusement machines in a travelling fair. He must've been seventeen or eighteen when he had his first fit. I heard my Uncle telling my Aunt about it, altho' I missed the details as they were talking low, the way the Irish do about sickness and death. He'd fallen down in the garden when he was picking raspberries, and they thought it was sunstroke at first. When he went into convulsions, tho', they knew it was something else. Scared the women. His sister Wee Anne wouldn't talk about it at all when I asked her.

I was warned not to accept a ride on his motorcycle or

let him drive the tractor. My Uncle just said simply that Billy wasn't all there.

He seemed normal enough to me. He continued to brag about his drinking and his women whenever we met, and in the treehouse he showed how much bigger his cock had become since riding the arse off that country woman from Skerry in the ditch the other night. He squeezed it until the veins were throbbing with blood, gave it a few savage jerks, relaxed, then resumed a more easy rhythm, all the while detailing his session with the country woman. As I watched I remembered him coming home late that night, singing "The Wild Colonial Boy" as he came through the plantation of beech trees, passed below my window, and continued through the darkness up the lane to his father's cottage. I supposed at the time he was just happy with drink or putting up a big bravado to show he wasn't afraid of the dark or any banshees, say.

I was waiting for him to ejaculate when he rolled up his eyes, uttered a small moan and fell backwards through the thicket of cane branches that girdled the tree some twenty feet from the ground. I panicked and scrambled down via the secret route and found him lying on his back in the long grass like he was dead. Just as I started to plead with him to be alive please he opened his eyes and let go his familiar sly laugh.

What happened, I said to him, you, you.... I had a fit, he said, know what that is? No, I said, I don't. Well, he said, that's a fit. I went along with this but somehow I wasn't convinced. I'd blacked out myself the first time I'd played with myself and I knew it wasn't anything special.

That's the thing, see. Billy used his reputation to scare people, to get power over them. He wasn't intimidated or humbled by his affliction, because he saw that others were. Other than a bit of amnesia, what were the consequences? None, apparently. Since some of the fits were quite mild, you were never sure if he was faking or what.

It was like that the day him and his sister Wee Anne and me were walking through the trees near the abandoned tennis court when he started acting odd, not making any sense. He fell down, convulsing in an obscene manner, just like he was dramatising his session with the Kerry woman. Wee Anne became quite distraught, saying we had to put a pencil between his teeth to keep him from biting his tongue, and then she ran off. I was quite unnerved too because he had his big camping knife on him and he was quite fond of trying frighten me. So as his convulsions subsided, I said to him, come on, Hearkness, quit faking. He lay on the path with his eyes closed, flecks of white froth issuing from the edges of his mouth. I walked off as if unconcerned and hid for a few minutes behind a tree before showing myself again. He was on his feet by then and as I approached I said, you fooled your sister that time. There was an odd, faraway look in his eyes, and he said, I just fainted. Oh, I said, is that it, I thought you were just faking. No, he said, I fainted. You should try it sometime. What for, I said. Better than a woman, he said.

Epilepsy. Better than a woman. For years this sexual matrix has lingered in my mind as a promise of liberation from the bondage of pussy and heartbreak. I meant to have further discussions on the subject with The Wild Colonial Boy but unfortunately he was killed shortly thereafter when he lost control of his motor cycle and was tossed headfirst with his date into a stone dyke.

The Idiot

WHAT ARE YOU? HE THUNDERED, circling the desk on which Nipper stood. Nipper refused to speak, either through fear or sullen determination, which was odd because he was the biggest arse licker in the class. James looked at the others, but they were uncaring, eager to join in on the humiliation of Nipper, and were just waiting for Dom to rouse them into a choir of condemnation. First, though, Dom would get Nipper to say the fatal words.

Dom was bald and the light from the ceiling reflected in a yellow aura on his shining cranium. He had a moustache but that was all the hair he had, except when he forgot to shave, which happened occasionally for no explicable reason, as Dom was meticulously clean on all accounts and drilled cleanliness into his students with a religious zeal. His blue eyes were killing, and James feared them, as did the others, because the challenge was often too great. Dom did not teach by kindness and benign indulgence: fear, humiliation, and a blow to the back of the head were his academic credentials.

Nipper stood on the desk like a slave at a Roman auction, his hands clenched into a cup before his crotch, as if he expected this humble gesture would catch his urine when it came. His face was red, like his ears which stood out in comic relief, even though his mother had taped them to the side of his skull when he was a child. But why had Dom picked on him, James wondered. No one else in the class knew the answer to the question either....

Dom was still circling, muttering below his breath, his head shuddering, his teeth grinding, mad at himself, the world, and the God who created it. It was a familiar ritual, one in which Dom would work himself into a frenzy, sometimes exploding into invective, other times fading into disinterest... if one was lucky. Nipper was not going to be lucky. Lost your tongue, fool? hissed Dom, stopping. Nipper's protruding ears twitched, his cheeks grew redder. Dom's voice dropped to a near whisper: it seems I will have to tell you what you are, McVicar. The other youths exchanged looks and deepened their sadistic smiles. Dom's blue eyes were locked onto Nipper's. *You are an idiot!* Dom suddenly shouted. *Say it!* Nipper's mouth trembled but the words wouldn't come. Dom gave him a swift lash with the blackboard pointer on the back of the legs. *Say it!* Nipper flinched but retained his ramrod stance. Dom recommenced a slow circling. Oh McVicar, he said contemptuously, there are imbeciles in this world, but they can't help what they are, and there are morons, and they can't help what they are either, but you, McVicar, you are the most quintessential of them all, *you are an idiot,* and by God if you are going to be an *idiot,* then you will acknowledge being an *idiot....*

James knew Nipper was anything but tough, yet he was surprised that he hadn't caved in immediately and started blubbering. Was it the inarticulation of fear or some new found fortitude? As he watched, he wondered when his turn would come, when would he be made to stand on his desk, proclaim himself to be what he knew most definitely *he* wasn't.... Now Dom was slicing the air with the pointer, and Nipper's face grew more pained. Briefly, his eyes swivelled towards James, who, much to his discomfort, realized he was smiling along with all the others. In that moment he knew he had betrayed Nipper, even though Nipper had never been anything but the butt of his jokes, a subject of easy torment.

I am an idiot. The admission surprised him, surprised them all, surprised even Dom in mid-stroke, and a silence filled the classroom as everyone remained in tableaux until

Nipper, reclaiming his dignity, stepped down from his desk. Where do you think you are going, McVicar? *Precisely?* Nipper brushed his hands against the fabric of his blazer, nervously removing their sweat. I said I was an idiot, sir, he said, and now I want to be excused. Dom turned away dismissively, said, you will stand with your face in the corner until I say otherwise. Nipper nodded, but instead of obeying, walked slowly but surely out the door as Dom stood by, strangely impotent, spinning the pointer like a circus performer executing a poorly conceived trick. When the door closed, a murmur passed through the room, but was quickly stilled when Dom snapped out of his trance.

For the rest of the lesson, as they worked with their heads to their desks, James was aware of Dom's slow patrol of the aisles. He wondered where Nipper had gone, and why he hadn't returned. He wondered what he was going to say to him after school when they cycled back to their village. Perhaps Nipper would ride by himself. Perhaps he'd already gone, deserted the school, defied the rules, decided to take his chances with the Headmaster in the morning. Or perhaps he'd gone ahead to the Dressing Rooms, because there was a rugger practice that afternoon, and Nipper, whatever his faults, was a good kicker.

The footsteps stopped right behind James and he was aware of Dom's breathing, the slight animal coarseness of it, as if the chalk dust from the blackboard was in his lungs, or he was anticipating the practice of the Under XIV squad. A glow came into James' neck as the short hairs uncoiled. Dom was leaning over, almost touching... what, precisely, is *that* you are drawing? James' mouth was dry. He said, a dolmen. Dom grunted, then said, why are you drawing a dolmen? James said, as an illustration of how the Irish used to bury their kings. James could feel Dom's hand on his shoulder. Very good, said Dom, patting him, and then moved on, his measured footsteps like an echo of the pats James could still feel on his stiffened shoulder.

Later James learned that Dom had taken liberties with Nipper in the Rugby Pavilion after practice one afternoon, had made overtures to buggery, but Nipper had resisted.

Also, he learned that Dom's nickname really stood for "Dead On Me" and not his bald cranium. With this information and the new perspective it formed, James realized there was nothing unique in being an idiot.

The Hunger

ANNE FELT SICK, BUT STILL WOULDN'T EAT anything,
even when her mother scolded her, said she was wasting
away to a shadow, why didn't she see the doctor because
there was something definitely wrong, how many more
days could she miss from school, she'd lose her job, they'd hire
another teacher and then where would they all be? In the
next room, her father jolted out of his slumber with a shout,
and he turned up the TV to rail against the clip about Seamus
"The Budgie" McVoy who was now into the twenty-sixth
day of his fast as a protest to the conditions in The Maze. As
her father cursed the Fenian bastard prima-donna Anne rose
from the kitchen table and went to the door of the sitting
room where she stood watching as the camera closed in on
McVoy's sunken, bearded face, and the sad eyes which had
those lovely pin-points of light. He looked like a rock star
or, God help him, Jesus. Her father's raging hate became a
babble of inconsequential noise as she repeated the number,
26, twenty-six days without food, 26, her very age no less.
The report ended, but she could still see McVoy's face as an
after-vision, and the history of his case scrolled past in its
familiar chronology. They said he was a *super grass*, that's
why he was in solitary, said he would betray his own mother, never mind the IRA, but none of that mattered to her.
McVoy was just a victim of circumstance, like many of the
children she taught who couldn't sleep at night without

wetting the bed, or coming to school with a knife.

Her father was talking to her, telling her to wake up and bring him his bottle of stout and his medicine, his back was killing him and he could hardly move his hand. She came partially out of her trance and regarded him in benign disbelief, his shrunken arthritic body buried deep in his old armchair, the chair that was as old as the shipyard he'd worked in, the chair he never left except to visit the lavatory or his shrine. His shrine was in the front room, the room with a glimpse of Belfast Lough, and consisted of a silk tapestry depicting King Billy crossing the Boyne River, sword extended, with the date 1690 and the war cry *No Surrender*. Beside the mantelpiece was the upper half of a tailor's dummy which wore the orange sash and the black bowler hat on its symbolic head. When one of his cronies came by he would hobble in here and turn on the electric fire and they would talk about the horses, the weather, the Troubles, the Queen, football and boxing. He was no longer allowed to eat bread with dripping, but fadge with a drop of butter was just fine.

Just what ails ye, Anne darlin', he said to her, and she turned away, said, nothing, daddy. In the kitchen the liver was being eaten by the dog, a rotund little creature with short legs, named Rinty after the celebrated light-weight who used to sing "When Irish Eyes Are Smiling" after all his fights, win or lose. As she recovered a bottle of Guinness from below the sink, her mother drew her hands from the water and gripped her shoulder, said, what's the matter with you, girl? If I didn't know any better, I'd say you were in love. Anne could feel warm water soaking through her blouse as her mother's wet fingers continued to dig into her shoulder, and the peculiar nature of it, the small heat that it was, caused her to relax, and in so doing, almost swoon. She dropped into a chair and leaned on the table and laughed while her mother continued to scold her, talk about lack of iron, and the girl they both knew who died of leukaemia. Look at Rinty! Anne said. He's getting so fat he won't be able to jump out the wee window any more! Her mother said you know Mrs. White is expecting you to go with them and the children to America next summer, and you'll need your strength. Anne said, I'm going to my room, mummy, I have to prepare my lesson. Her mother dried her hands, said, are you going back tomorrow? I'll believe it when I see it, girl. Anne said, yes, tomorrow.

Her mother opened the stout and the smell of it made her nauseous, but she managed to get upstairs into her room before convulsing in a series of dry, futile heaves. When they passed, she lit the scented candle she'd bought the last time she'd been with the children in America, on the healing holiday for Protestants and Catholics alike, the holiday away from this city and its sectarian nightmare, and withdrew the folder from its secret place below the carpet and placed it on her desk. The folder contained a series of newspaper clippings about Seamus McVoy, the man she had never met, but had seen many times on the television and in the papers. Here was his picture, his face without the beard, his face before the hunger strike, the face of the darling whom they said was a killer and a traitor....

Love — what was love? In the lonely solitude of her shrine, her heart ached for the wasting man in his solitary cell somewhere beyond the city. She bowed her head, her dry mouth opening for her white knuckles as she waited for tomorrow, the 27th day.

The Water Wheel

THERE HE IS, MY TORMENTING MENTOR, beckoning from the stone gate that leads into the woods, and can I do anything but run to his side like a dumb animal? Once we are in the trees, the light changes and the wind hisses through the arterial foliage, and I trot by his side, happy to be included in his sophisticated enterprise, whatever it should be. Perhaps he will uncover his rifle from some hidden refuge in the roots of a mature beech and we will hunt for rabbits. Or perhaps we will climb into the trees and investigate the nests... but no, he leads me to the stream which cuts through the woods in a shallow series of cascades like an abandoned stairway.

I can hear it before I can see it, the hypnotic fump fump fump of the blades as the water strikes them in its endless chorus. We stand on the bank as he points in pure modesty at his latest handiwork, a small water wheel, which tosses gleaming shards of water into the holes of sunlight that pattern the stones and the moss. I stare in awe, as the small wheel revolves, ingenious in its simplicity, magical in its motion. He has damned the stream with a few stones, directed its flow with an old piece of gutter, crossed two boards for the blades, suspended them between two stakes pounded into the bed of the stream. As the strange glow of creation tingles my skin, I know I will emulate my mentor, will build many such water wheels, locate them in the hidden pools of the stream as secret artifacts for those in search of mystery.

As we sit on the bank listening and watching, deep below the giant beech trees, he lights a cigarette, and after a couple of inhalations, offers it to me. I shake my head, but his eyes remain on mine, his smile faintly mocking. The cigarette remains poised, an obstacle between me and the water wheel, and I long to remove it, regain my trance. My hand accepts the cigarette, although my mind accepts only the water wheel, and my hand moves it slowly to my mouth, so, for the first time, I am sucking the acrid juice of nicotine.

There is another sound blending with that of the waterwheel. Like a fox my mentor hears it, and descends stealthily into the stream, crawls over the stones in search of his prey. As he rises from his stoop, he uncups his hands and I see a frog, its olive body mottled with black spots. He motions me to join him and I drop the butt and slide slowly down the bank. With a crafty smile he places the frog on an elevated stone where it remains frozen, caught in my mentor's spell, unable to leap to freedom, unable to escape the chorus of the water wheel. He finds a patch of rushes and removes a dead straw, which he trims to size before inserting one end in the frog's mouth. He then blows through the straw and slowly the frog's yellow stomach inflates. I think this cruel ritual must have a quick ending but no, the stomach continues to expand until it is larger than the frog itself, so that the small amphibian appears to be clinging to the slippery yellow sphere that was its stomach.

My mentor ceases his labours and indicates that I should take the straw. But I cannot move, because my trance is complete. I too have been trapped by the water wheel.

The Right Way to Drink Tea

THE WOMEN COULDN'T STAND HIS ANCIENT CUS-
TOMS, and hissed when he poured his tea into his saucer
and supped from it like an animal. In their attempt to ac-
quire breeding, such country excesses were no longer ac-
ceptable, but I loved his tricks, and he bounced me on his
lap, bade me pour my tea into its saucer and blow on it,
which I did quite gleefully. The women scowled and cried
shame, then chuckled ruefully as they watched me sup
noisily, my manners ruined forever.

But it was his ticking heart that I loved best, and would
lie with my ear pressed against his waistcoat, enraptured by
its Swiss precision. Oh his heart wasn't like my heart or any
other heart, the heart of my mother or my father, it was the
secret heart of my grandfather, the big man who owned
the estate, the flax mill, and the whole world it seemed. His
moustache tickled my ear as he bade me learn the country
words, the old Gaelic nonsense like *shugh... shughhh* with a
guttural roll, *shugh*, the muddy spot in a field where the cattle dug up the sod and the rain did the rest, *shugh* the state
of nearly every *slap* in every field, *shugh*, the very condi-
tion of Ireland it seemed.

I followed him into the fields to inspect the cattle, and
we checked to see that none had escaped through a gap in
the hedge, or forced an exit through a fence. I watched him
count the heads with his thorn stick, and bark commands

to his collie who raced to round up stragglers... or the swallows she could never catch. When my small rubber boots got stuck in the mud, he lifted me up, saved me from the *shugh* and carried me through the *slap* onto the *lonin*, which was just a rough stone track for the big horses and their carts.

One day he went up to the meadow beside the flax dams and didn't come back for his tea and they sent someone looking for him. He was lying where he had fallen, dead of a heart attack. They took the big white door from the Corn Room, the one with the set of conversion tables painted on it, and used that to carry him back to the house. It took four of them because he was a big man, and the weight wasn't all in his boots. They set the door on a couple of saw horses, where the women shaved him and dressed him in his best suit. He was down to my size now. I put my ear to the side of his waistcoat and much to my bewilderment, it was silent. Gone to heaven, the women said, and he wouldn't be needing his watch.

Gone to heaven indeed. A few years later we were up in the meadow ploughing it for potatoes and it must have been the last time we used horses for it too, because I remember I was allowed to take the reins and try my hand at turning a furrow. Shiela was there, running after seagulls this time, and I turned up something other than worms: my grandfather's gold watch. I still have it today and every time I hear it ticking, I remember the man who showed me the right way to drink tea.

The Bull

HE BOUGHT THE BULL, and by God what a bull it was, good enough for all two hundred of those heifers, and any more the neighbours had too, if they had the money... or a gap in their hedges. It was black like the coal in the Furnace Room, so black that its flanks flashed sheets of silver, silver like the big ring in its nose. He got it from a man on the other side of Bellaghy, where the drums beat day and night in the summer and they can drink you under the table any time you think you're able. This bull was big too, size of a horse and heavier, big boned and Irish to the hilt. I tell you, I never saw a bull like it and I've visited many a farm since, sir, buying livestock all over Ulster, and as often as not in the South too. The cods on it, Jesus you'd need two hands and a shovel....

My father put him in the big field where you can see Slemish Mountain from and that evening he was out of there and all the heifers were with him, swarming up the lonin in a pure riot, sir. I was in the kitchen having my tea when I heard the thunder of them coming between the walls of the garden and the mill, and I looked out the window and there he was, his big head with the chopped horns just visible above the hedge. The heifers were going mad, running through the hen yard, sending the birds into the holly bushes, some of them drinking from the stream, some of them eating the hedge and everything else that was green. I ran up the way, got Hearkness and his sister, the pig killer's weans, and we managed to corner the bull at the midden. Oh he was dangerous, make no mistake about it, and we had a hard time diverting him into the Dipping Yard, because he had a mind just to run over the top of us, which he did anyway when we put him in the shed and he kicked the bloody the door down and me beneath it, ruined my shirt, my pants, bloodied my face, and I think I still have a scar from it. But there was nowhere for him to go, as the gate on the yard was iron and even a bull can't break that. Of course the heifers were all over Hell's Acre but I just let Hearkness round them up. When my father came back he called the Vet and the Vet tried to give him a sleeping pill but the bull would have none of that and I thought we were going to have to shoot the bugger, because he was completely unmanageable, no field could hold him, and he was forever leading the heifers all over the countryside.

We had to sell him to McAllister, who was bringing in young heifers from the South, but I think he regretted it. I think he did. I think that bull wrecked his van, put a dent in the side of his Rover, made a mess of Mrs. McAllister's garden. I think they had to shoot him, and what a shame that was, for he was a magnificent creature, like something from the jungle. I can still see the cods on him, and the steam coming out of his nostrils. I think my father lost money on him, but he was glad enough to see him go, as a couple of the heifers were badly injured, broken legs I seem to recall. It's a strange thing that, isn't it? The way heifers just allow themselves to be put in a field, fattened up, then auctioned off to the slaughterhouse. I'm sure that won't go on forever. I'm sure one day they'll all break out again, the whole bloody lot of them, but I'll tell you this: it will take a bull to lead them.

Cromwell

FOR SENTIMENTAL REASONS he'd decided to take the boat instead of flying to London, as he'd taken the night crossing many times in his youth. He enjoyed seeing the shipyards and whatever vessels were under construction, the whole industrial might of it, the glory of Belfast. But as the ferry broke its moorings and started into the Lough, a thick fog came up obscuring everything, so that the big gantries and the yards that built the *S.S. Titannic* and *H.M.S Ark Royal* passed by in a series of phantom shapes unrecognizable as history or current fact.

He was alone at the starboard rail, vexed but not disappointed, because the experience of being in the fog was a novelty in itself. He could hear the other passengers getting rowdy in the bar, and he thought he'd have a couple himself before he turned in. He shivered, tightened the belt on his overcoat, brushed the moisture from his eyebrows with the back of his hand, then admired the white furrow of surf breaking from the bow, which was about all there was to see. Then, just above him, the ferry sounded its horn, which startled him more than the appearance of another passenger. As the echoes from the horn faded across the widening plane of the hidden Lough, the newcomer lit a cigarette and leaned on the rail, looking pensively into the fog as if he somehow had the ability to see right through it. At first Thompson thought the man might be a crewman because his jacket was like a stevedore's, with leather yokes on the shoulders. As Thompson turned away, he saw what the man was looking at: a large ship which was materializing from the silver wall like an apparition. Although it was at anchor, it had the illusion of movement, and as they passed, the military gray ugliness of it was unnerving. It was mostly a hull with little superstructure, like a navy supply ship which was ready for the scrapyard. There was no name on the stern, and no navigation lights, and it was close enough to hit with a beer bottle. We must be off course, said Thompson spontaneously, assuming no one would anchor such a vessel in the main shipping channel.

The man looked at him, then tossed his cigarette towards the water and laughed shortly. Are ye American? he said in the familiar sing song Belfast accent. No, said Thompson. He didn't elaborate, because the fascination of the unmarked ship still held him in its curious spell. That's *The Cromwell*, said the man. The mass of it, blending as it did with the iridescent particles of moisture, seemed to suck the sound from the ferry, so that the engines grew muffled and revelry in the bar became more distant. They were passing the bow, and there was no name there either, so Thompson said, it must've been pulled up from the bottom. The man said, that'd be a good place for it. They watched in silence as it dissolved back into the fog and even when it was completely gone, the image of it persisted strongly in Thompson's mind. What was it? he said, I mean, what was it used for? A prison, said the man, and Thompson, surprised, said, a *prison* ship? Still is, said the man. Some people call it *Hotel Thatcher*, others *The Love Boat*. But it's *The Cromwell* and if yer Irish, ye know who Cromwell is.... The man was facing him now, his face hard, challenging, and Thompson wished he smoked, wished he had an exotic cigarette to offer him, or even a mickey to share. You're not a Brit, are ye? the man said to him, and Thompson said, I don't know what I am any more. It was time to walk away, go to the lounge, join the crowd, leave this all behind, but he was riveted to the deck. The man was close now, so close the hairs in his nostrils were visible, and the dank sweat of the fog on his sunken cheeks. Put a black suit on him and he was a priest, a stern apostle of morality, put a flak jacket on him and he was... just another citizen of Belfast.

Brown Waters From the Moss

THIS UNCLE WAS THE ONE who was supposed to have got a woman in trouble and was then shipped off to Rhodesia for a couple of years by his parents and when he came back he married my Aunt Rebecca. It was a good match on the face of it, except the parents were elderly and had to be nursed, and then Rebecca found out she would never be able to have children and this drove her to distraction. She went down to the river behind the house and threatened to drown herself and Uncle Roy had a terrible time dissuading her as she was standing in the rapids and the flood was on, the brown water from the moss, all that rain in the hills, the full Spring weight of it. He ended up wading out into the water after her, and then the doctor gave her something that kept her in bed for a week. I didn't witness this but I knew the river, I knew the spot, and every time I passed it, I thought about them standing in that brown water, so serene most of the year, but at that time tumbling and pitching through the rapids dirty brown and frothing like draught ale.

Roy had the spartan tastes of a presbyter. He didn't drink and the only smoking he did was when he lit a pipe in the evening to read the newspaper or listen to the radio. When his parents died and passed on their considerable wealth, none of this changed; there was an even rhythm to his life that was as simple as the ticking of the clock above the kitchen stove. But who would inherit his estate? This was always a subject of debate by others, and there were pretenders, some subtle, others openly crass like the fundamentalist preacher who occasionally dropped by and offered prayers in the dining room which required all present to drop to their knees, eyes closed, minds surrendered. Rebecca knew his game but sustained a mask of deference in his company, allowed her lips to say *Amen* when he finished his ritual. Rebecca was more taken by Leslie, a youth who was the son of a policeman who lived in a cottage beside the bridge and who was always available for odd jobs. Roy liked him too, even took the dog and went shooting with him, and always had him in when the haying came. I knew Les. He could sit on his bicycle without one foot on the ground, both hands in his pockets and have a conversation with you. A straight arrow, balanced and true. Nothing devious or syncophantic about him, and, except for his lowly station in life, he was very similar to Roy in nature. His mother was paralysed, supposedly as a result of complications from his birth, and spent most of her time at the back of the cottage sitting in her wheel chair listening to the river. Rebecca spoke very sympathetically about her, as if they both shared an affliction that made them even.

They're both gone now, Uncle Roy and Aunt Rebecca, although I can still hear their voices in my head. Of course I wasn't really their nephew, I was just adopted as one out of kindness... and necessity. I can hear the river too, the sound always in my ears, the favourite sound of my mother, god rest her soul. I went to Africa myself, did alright, and I'm thinking about returning to that place by the brown waters and claiming my inheritance.

Point-of-View

FROM WHERE I STAND, all the ladies look much the same. I see a lot of varicose veins, and suspenders, and sometimes I can see knickers. Hughie says we come from knickers but I can't believe this, because if that was so we would get sucked into the toilet every time we go pooh. Sometimes I walk below the table and stick my head in there just to see, but most of them cuff me away, or lock their knees around my head and squeeze me until I'm crying, which makes them laugh, and when they laugh I get angry, so angry I dance with rage.

This is why I attacked mama the other day when she was picking shamrocks on the lawn. She was just my size the way she was kneeling and I came up behind her very quietly and hit her on the back with all my strength, both my fists tight together the way Hughie showed me, and mama screamed. I laughed, oh how I laughed, but when she stood up I thought oh mama's angry, she's going to cry, so my laughing went away and crying just came from somewhere secret. I ran to her for comfort and she gathered me in her arms and her nice smell was as always and I thought she was going to sing to me, sing about the shamrock. But she bite me, bite me on my arm where it joins my body, bite me worse than I ever bit her and the blood came out the tiny holes and this was worse than anything, worse than being crushed between their legs, the ladies' legs I mean.

When I tried to run away, she lifted me by the straps of my pants and carried me into the house and shut me in my room but I can climb out of my crib after I finish crying. I can do this for days now, it's easy. The window was open and it was just the same thing, out the crib, out the window, and down by the fence I see Hughie who is twice me and goes anywhere he likes, as far as the broken building he says was his house before the bomb fell. Hughie has a red lollipop, sticks it through the fence, then pulls it back when I try to get a lick, does this to see me dance, which I almost do, because he keeps doing it. But Hughie is then merciful for Hughie has a new trick he wants me to see and he passes the lollipop through the fence I can never climb... and I took it, thought, this is mine now.

Hughie took out Johnny and squirted his pee up high, it was so funny, he was able to squirt it over the wall that's bigger than both of us, even if I could stand on his shoulders. He squirted, laughed, I licked, laughed, he squirted and I licked, the both of us laughed, oh we laughed until the man's face sat on the wall and his face was angry, worse than the face in the sky at night, and Hughie had to run for it and the lollipop is mine forever.

Later I fell asleep on the floor, my thumb in my mouth, or perhaps that was before I woke up, remembered about the ladies. They were all at the table again, playing cards, some of them knitting, and when I asked for a drink mama tried to tape my ears to the side of my head because the one with the fat legs said it would make me pretty, I would grow up to be like them, and I thought, if I do grow bigger, please God make things different.

Cortina

HE LIKED THIS CORTINA best of the whole pack, even better than its duplicate parked outside the house, or any of the others he'd stolen in the last two years. He watched Ellis park it in front of the other one, then let the curtain drop back, before descending the stairs and taking his leather jacket from the coat rack in the hall. As he checked his hair in the small vanity mirror on the rack, Cliona shouted over the noise of the TV, if you're not back from the pub by eight I'm goin' to the Bingo, Brendan. Brendan allowed a small sneer to cross his baby-fat face, tightened the belt on his jeans, leaned leftwards and looked in the sitting room. Cliona was reclining on the sofa, doing her nails. Her back was to the door; he was going to say something, thought the better of it, zipped up his jacket and went out the front door into the cold night air.

Ellis was standing in the street, his hands deep in the pockets of his parka. He nodded to Brendan who said, have ye swapped the plates back? Ellis nodded again, removed a screw driver from his pocket, flipped it in his hand like a trick shooter. She's all tuned, ready to go? said Brendan. Like a bomb, said Ellis, and chuckled. How much do I owe ye? said Brendan, eying both vehicles in the sparse light thrown by the nearby street lamp. On the house, Elvis, said Ellis, and for the first time both men made eye contact. Brendan could see the mockery in those hooded eyes, sensed the contempt that was masked by the shadow that divided his bony face like a Janus, and in that moment knew that he hated Ellis. Like a preordained ritual, both men tossed a set of keys to one another, exchanging cars. As Brendan got into the new one, Ellis followed him, said be careful. Brendan ignored him, started the engine, engaged the clutch and roared off down the street. As he dialled in the local rock station, he could smell Ellis in the car, that after-shave Ellis used, those cigarettes Ellis smoked, but he knew before he checked the ash-tray there would be no butts, no careless clues, because Ellis was meticulous.

The car had a lot of snap to it and the trim was great as it came out of the corners. They all looked the same but this one was different and it was a shame that he was going to have to part with it. He felt like taking it for a run, maybe up the Antrim Road, or west on the Motorway, but he knew he had to stop at "The Imperial" first, have a drink. He felt tight, impotent, like an animal denied the chance to kill. He parked in the lot beside the chapel, locked the door, then crossed the street and went into the pub and ordered a pint of Guinness. He stood at the bar and drank it, talked to no one, although he recognized most of the people. He certainly recognized Joe Sullivan, who was supposed to be a Brigade Commander in the Officials, even though he was an old man now. Sullivan was sitting in the corner drinking with some cronies and very briefly his eyes turned and locked with Brendan's, and when Brendan drained his drink, he found he was tenser than ever, so he walked down the street, had a couple more pints in "McGinty's" before picking up the Cortina again and heading for his destination. The route had been carefully planned to avoid known Army and RUC roadblocks but the drink was making him feel rebellious and question the wisdom of it. Instead of going to "Simple Simon's", the well-known disco at the back of Rhodesia Street that was a favourite of off-duty soldiers and Protestants and students of both religions, he stopped outside "The Sacred Heart" pub and knocked off two more pints, this time with Jamison chasers. A drunken woman whom he knew slightly fixed her greedy eyes on him and he smiled at her thinly, said he would buy her a drink, but didn't. By now he was no longer tense, and when he got back in the Cortina, he didn't give a damn about "Simon's" and decided he'd drive back home and have it out with Cliona, the slag. This was nearly his undoing because he almost drove into a road-block at the bottom of the Falls Road and was saved only because a tanker truck came up and he was able drop back and take a side street. When he got back to his house, the other Cortina was gone, as expected, and when he checked inside, Cliona was also gone, which, when he thought about it, was also as expected.

He knew where she was, and he drove the short distance to the "Clifton Working Man's Club" which is where they had the Bingo every Saturday night, a charity run by the priests. He pulled into the kerb right behind the other Cortina that was parked outside the hall and for a moment sat drumming his fingers on the steering wheel as he let the engine idle. Ellis — how he hated that bastard! He'd never trusted him, right from the start. Ellis was a cross-over, he'd been a Prod but converted for his last wife, and he couldn't be trusted no matter how good of a mechanic he was.

Brendan shut off the engine, left the keys in the ignition, reached below the dash, found the two freshly installed green wires and twisted their ends together. He then got out of this Cortina and advanced to the other, removed the duplicate keys he'd previously had made, and unlocked the door. The smell was in this one too, the Ellis smell, but it was richer, more of a perfume than an after-shave. He looked in the ashtray: there were two fresh butts, one of them with lipstick. Brendan laughed, and it was the hard laugh of a man who drinks without getting drunk. He reached for the keys, then hesitated before turning the ignition, a new suspicion arriving his mind. He was tense again, his body rigid with the sense of death, so he turned the key quickly, knowing it made little difference one way or the other.

Back in his house, sitting on the same sofa Cliona had been on earlier, he watched the Late News and the report of the massive explosion at the Clifton Working Man's Club, a man and a woman dead in the car that did it, a dozen more injured and dying, this, the third car bomb in a month, the shocking outrage of it, but Brendan knew all this, had heard it before, would hear it again, because there were plenty more Cortinas waiting to be stolen.

The Field of the Poets

IF THERE WAS A WILDER PART OF ULSTER, Thompson had never seen it, and it was misting from the low moving cloud right to the place where his car had stalled. He got out, raised the hood and saw immediately that the engine had over-heated from lack of water in the radiator after that long climb up from the glen onto the moss. Where was he? He hadn't a clue, really, because he'd just been touring about in his rented car, rediscovering places from his youth... and now, what was he going to do? Wait forever for another motorist? He was on a narrow road on a rolling plateau of heather which stretched for miles in all directions until it died in the overcast. It was little more than a donkey track, and even they didn't travel it any more.

The drizzle was coming heavier now, so he got back into the car until it passed, and when the sun broke through again he marvelled at the changeability of the atmosphere, the sense of the sea never being very far away. He rolled down the window and as he did so, saw a large deer cross the road and start grazing casually on the lower side of the slope. He got out again, and the sound of the door closing startled the deer, which bounded off in the familiar zig zag coursing of graceful leaps until it disappeared behind the remains of a stone wall. Thompson was impressed; this was the first wild deer he'd seen in Ireland, although they were common enough where he lived on the other side of the ocean. He stood watching and listening, but the deer didn't reappear, although he thought he could hear a stream, and this brought him new hope. There was nothing to collect water in, though, except a hubcap which he proceeded to pop off the front wheel with the tire iron before descending the slope towards the ruin.

The landscape was like one of those paintings his Uncle used to have in his dinning room, except there were no shaggy Highland cattle to be seen. But the light was the same, the panorama of leaden skies with the occasional gleaming break through which the sun poured in giant, shifting spokes. When he came to the wall, he expected to see the deer again but was surprised to see a young woman apparently waiting for him. He was surprised for another reason too: she was a striking beauty, tall and lean, with the dramatic face of a model, but unmistakably Irish when she removed her beret and shook out her full, rolling red hair. Thompson stopped in his tracks, glanced around, thinking there must be a photographer present, more than a little shy as was his habit when encountering a woman alone.

Did you see the deer? he said, and she turned, followed his eyes, before shaking her head. I saw one, he said foolishly, it ran this way... but I guess it kept going. She was looking at the hubcap, which he was jigging nervously, and he said, the car's overheated, I thought maybe there was a stream nearby. Yes, she said, you can get water here. There was a silence. She looked away, and he said, this is the most beautiful spot... what's it called? She gave her head a toss, pushed her hair behind her shoulder, jangling her silver bracelets, said, didn't you know? This is *The Field of the Poets*. As she said this he noticed what indeed appeared to be a field, a long green sward between the heather which ran for a quarter of a mile or more from the wall and was dotted with boulders. He had noticed these boulders but that they should be considered as *deliberate* hadn't occurred to him... but now, as he surveyed the arrangement, he could see that they extended from where he was standing in a fan shape. He said, is this a megalithic site? She said, it's very old, all the ancient poets are buried here, Finn the Fair, his son Ossian, Mael the Druid, all of them.... As he heard this, Thompson tried to count them, but there was an abstraction to them at their distant extremities. He said, I've never heard of this place... surely it's just a legend, just another Irish romanticism like the Giant's Causeway. She dug her hands into her tweed walking jacket, drew it tightly to her as she smiled and shrugged, and Thompson felt a thrill pass through him, the sort he hadn't experienced in years, that spasm that is both a signal and a sentence. As his eyes passed over her, her boots with their buckles, her long pleated skirt, her green blouse and the Celtic jewellery, her beauty screamed at him while he struggled to remain polite, dignified, not crudely impressed.

The light faded as the hole in the clouds closed and *The Field* lost its green vibration, blended with the olive hue of the moor and the sensation of imminent rain returned. He said, are you a tourist like myself? And she said, I'm a friend of the poets. He laughed, thought, she's playing with me, perhaps I'm as much a mystery to her as she is to me. He said, I can imagine you would come to this place quite often because it's so... so, beautiful. She said, I do.

I will, I will. Deep, fast bullets of rain came in a brief shower. He felt like fainting as they struck his upturned face. She pulled on her beret, said, there's a stream just yonder by that bit of bush. He could see the depression, a small black cut in the peat perhaps thirty yards away, but it seemed irrelevant. Yet he had no real excuse to linger and when he said thanks and set off for the stream, he began to plot ways to get her name, maybe even take her with him. How did she get there? Was she expecting someone? Was someone else in the vicinity? It took several trips back and forth from the stream to the car to bring the radiator back up and just precisely when she disappeared from the wall, he couldn't say. One time she was there watching him, the next she wasn't. He screwed cap back on, closed the hood, looked at the wall, no sign of her. He banged the hub cap back on, dropped the tire iron back in the trunk, looked again, still no sign of her. When he got in the driver's seat and turned the ignition and the car started, he was actually disappointed. He drove along the shoulder for a few yards, then stopped, thinking he should go and see if she needed a lift. Why not? It was the gentlemanly thing to do... even if he was less of a gentleman than he realized.

There was no one at the wall and no one in *The Field of the Poets*. As he wandered through the rocks, their weather-beaten surfaces were devoid of inscription, their arrangement ambiguous to Nature and Man. Yet the idea of it, the idea that an army of ghosts resided in this wild and splendid place, was intoxicating. The poetic soul of Ireland, the first articulation, the way of saying things, the character and the spirit, the shape of it, the knowing into the forgetting, the idea in the human forever, here, the idea, here, in the rolling air, in the warm wetness and the cold eternity, here, the stones....

We will, we will. She could be lying in the peat moss or moving through the heather and he still might not see her, he thought as he returned to the car. Ah... it was just as well. While he had a sense of loss, the accidental character of it was complete in its mystery, and perhaps it was just as well she had disappeared. And who knows? He might see her somewhere, perhaps in a magazine, her elegant arms and neck featuring the jewellery of the ancient princesses. As he let the engine idle, allowing it to recover its rhythm, the weather turned capricious again, the cloud dropping close to the moss and bringing the fine misting rain with it, obscuring the wall and the stones beyond it in another curtain.

He drove off and had gone only a short distance when the deer showed up ahead, trotting on the tarmac, and even when he sounded his horn, it seemed reluctant to leave the road. His speed dropped, the engine hiccuped when he missed a gear change, and once more the car stalled. He opened the door, a curse on his lips, but his indignation faded to admiration as he watched her veer from the road and cascade into the moss.

Teddy Boy

YOU YOUNG PUNKS THINK THE WORLD starts with you, but I tell you it doesn't, and didn't, and if you care to listen I'll tell you precisely where you come from. You're all Teddy Boys and don't know it, don't know the evolution of it, the first breath of it, and there's nothing worse than vanity without calculation. Think about it: you're just like the fella who fell in love with himself when he leaned over to take a drink and saw himself in the water.

Listen to me: I saw my first legitimate Ted the day I came up to Belfast to see Bill Haley and the Comets and that was a long time ago. Records were 78 rpm then, that's how far back it was. I'd just come off the platform to meet up with my pal Natch who, without saying a word of greeting, jerks his thumb backwards and over his shoulder I see him, the first real Teddy Boy in the flesh. Aw he was a classic, alright, completely orthodox in all respects: thick crepe-soled shoes, blue suede, of course; black stove-pipe trousers, Edwardian three-quarter jacket, the lapels hanging just above his knees, velvet collar, naturally; white Mississippi Gambler blouse with a lace tie, big knuckle-duster ring on his punching hand; side-burns and Tony Curtis lock hanging over his forehead, and when he wasn't sucking on a fag, he was chewing gum. I was in awe, and you would be too if you had seen him. Here he is studiously reading the Racing page in some local tabloid one foot crossed over the other as the pigeons scurry about looking for Christ-knows-what on the concrete floor and when Natch looks back at me, he nods slowly, smiles, then breaks into a nervous laugh. Oh yes — I'd come to the right place. These big city blokes didn't fool around. You see, Natch had thick soles and his pants were tight enough, but he favoured a cravat, something which struck me as odd, perhaps passé, although that word wasn't as yet in my repertoire. To be confronted by an all-out Ted was a bit unnerving, because as we start to walk away this one looks up from his paper, looks us over, and spits. It was provocative right enough, but what are you going to do? Call him on it in broad daylight with all the people running about and the police standing by the exit? So I knew he didn't think much of me. You see, I was rock 'n' roll, even though rock 'n' roll still hadn't made its mark on Ireland. I had a black jacket with gray chevron patterns, long lapels and a single button, the closest thing I could find to what Elvis or Gene Vincent might wear. Back home they called me a Ted but I was no Ted, as Ted was working-class, the latest in what was a long tradition of fashion thugs in the U.K. stretching back into the eighteenth century, and I was all-American, hopelessly caught in what I later recognized as The Cult of the Hip. So you just think about where that puts *you* in The Great Chain of Being. There's nothing new about a shaven head, no.

We hop a tram up Royal Avenue to the City Hall, where we disembark and hang around for awhile, looking at the tarts and anything else that passes, which, if they are men, are either *hards*, semi-Teds, or Teds outright, and there aren't many of the latter, not as legitimately Ted as the bloke we saw at the railway station. There are mutations, lots of them, everything from the gaberdine suits of the greyhound jockeys, and the other breed, the *student*, who always has the obligatory Queen's University scarf tied around the throat, the ends draped over the shoulders of his tweed jacket or oversized pullover. To be honest, I viewed these characters with a mixture of loathing and envy, as there was something of a middle-class pretentiousness about the pose, an effeminate aura that was only cancelled by the occasional undergraduate decadent, and fortunately we knew a few of those. But you know what I'm saying? Of course you do, you may be ignorant but you're not stupid. The women students weren't much different, and what we sought in that stream of humanity circling the City Hall was a *female* Ted, a girl who didn't wear any knickers and carried a frenchie in her purse. Just like you lot today. But there weren't any, of course; Teddy Boys were the ultimate precursor of what later became a big thing in rock 'n' roll, the bisexual sadist. Aw laugh, go ahead, but cast your mind around a bit and I think you can name a few. Anyway, so here we are, sitting on a bench at the hub of the city, smelling the lead and diesel of the traffic, seeing the odd carter clip clop past, an old gaffer who couldn't give a damn about fashion, sees only his horse's arse as he spits nicotine phlegm in contempt for the new world, here we are, two young bucks with no respect for anything except our mothers, here we are, toffed up and waiting for the night.

You think you've seen a rock 'n' roll concert or two, and I'm sure you have, but this was in the beginning, I'm saying, this was the *first*. The Comets were playing at the Opera House, and the place was packed, with a mob screaming outside, eager for a chance to riot as was the custom everywhere Bill Haley played in the U.K. that year. We had seats in the Gods and if you haven't been up there, in just such a building, you don't know what cheap is. The seating is tiered, so steep I'm thinking if I lean forward I'll go arse over end and fall clear into the orchestra pit in a slow swoon. From the moment Haley hits the stage with his kiss curl and f-slot guitar, the place is in total pandemonium, but you know all about that, things have got worse if anything these days. He rips through his famous set, including "See You Later Alligator," "Shake, Rattle & Roll," "Rock Around The Clock," "Thirteen Women And Only One Man In Town," more or less the way you could hear them on the 78. People are jumping up and down in their seats, the girls are screaming like they're at a funeral in Damascus, and it's all I can do to stop from throwing myself off the balcony. Was it the second song, or third, when people started dancing in the aisles?

Maybe it was when the bass player began to ride his big double bass fiddle or when the tenor sax man went down on his back for his solo, I don't know, but I know another real live Ted materialized a couple of rows below us and started dancing on his seat, real gone jive boogie and he didn't give a damn for the ushers who used their flashlights on him. It was incredible to see him, crouched over, his feet pedalling in high-speed intricacies, within a few feet of the railing, one wrong step and he was gone. The band, the Ted, the people out of their heads, jumping in their seats, dancing where they could, everywhere you looked, the new anarchy. Jesus, that guitar player, with his fast rockabilly licks, all bebop and country at the same time, it was enough to make you stuff school and head for Memphis, which is why I started playing guitar, and listen, I could show you young pups a thing or two and I'm not codding. But that aside, think about it, this was a historic moment: there's Haley whose small rhythm unit signalled the end of the dance orchestra, and there's Teddy Boy X, who signalled the beginning of British rock 'n' roll. You look at some of the early photos of the Beatles and the Stones, and you tell me if there isn't a bit of the Ted in them. You bet. Pure Teddy Boy culture might've passed with the fifties, but it lives on in the fashion foppery of the anglo rock and roller...and you, my friend.

After the concert, I had to go back to the station to catch the last train and stupidly chose to walk, and would you walk it tonight, except in a pack? I don't think so. They talk about Hamburg being a hard city, New York even, but they should try Belfast I think. Somewhere along the way we were challenged by a trio of *hards*. The leader had pretensions to being a Ted, but he wasn't the real thing, he wasn't a Ted completely. He had stove-pipes and greased hair, and his hard face was as ugly as the obscenities that came out of his mouth. I remember he wanted me, but he got Natch, who took him down to the pavement in a headlock. I danced with his cronies, a few feints, air punches, some talk, but the humiliation of their leader did them. They called Natch a queer because of his cravat, but you see, you can't always judge a man by his clothes. Remember that.

Ah, but these asides, these opinions, my friend, don't reveal the psychological dimensions of our poses in those days. Teds were viewed as hooligans, and you know the original Hooligan was an Irishman. I never went so far as to dye or perm my hair, as did many of the Teds, or did I carry a bicycle chain or a razor, as did many of the Teds. There were those who said Teddy Boys weren't Irish and they were right about that, but rock 'n' roll wasn't either, and listen, I wasn't a Ted. I wasn't but people kept calling me one and I'm sure many others were called the same, so there might be something to it; you could be Catholic, but it doesn't mean you walk around dolled up like a priest. When you see an old fart like me in the pub the next time, don't consider me irrelevant until you check out my wardrobe: there just might be a Teddy suit in there waiting for the next bastard with the guts to claim it.

Flash

EVERY MORNING THE MAN WOULD COME with his toast and hard-boiled egg and cup of tea and, if he was in favour, the man would let him have a look at the newspaper. What was the fellow's name? Mulrooney or Mulhaven or Mul something. He couldn't bloody remember. He would call him "M". Where the hell was M.? He was starving, and he couldn't do any work on an empty stomach. He sat on the edge of his bed, his red eyes taking in the contents of the room: an old easy chair by the gas fire, and a desk against the green wall where he did his studying. The problem was, he had to use his desk as a kitchen table to eat his meals at, and when he wasn't eating or studying, he had to use it as a workbench where he was constructing the *Singularity Machine*. It was still in pieces. He could see the soldering iron lying on an open book... was it his notes or what was it? He couldn't remember leaving it there like that last night. Some careless bastard must've been messing around with his stuff.

He rose, but went to the window instead. The glass had been painted green, so no one could spy, but someone had scratched a small peephole for looking outside. What he saw was a surprise: a jangle of industrial rooftops with a huge gantry towering in the background. What was this? Where was he? Had they moved him? This wasn't there yesterday. In his anger, he resolved to abandon his work. He would tell M. he wasn't going to put up with this, that he was through, they would have to find someone else, that was all there was to it.

He heard the key in the door and a moment later M. came in carrying a tray. M. kicked the door shut with his foot, paused, said, what's the matter, Professor? Bad night? Need to go to the lavatory? He set the tray on the desk, making room in the litter with a sweep of his large hand. His face was coarse with stubble, and as he smiled, his eyes drilled into the Professor until the Professor became confused, unsure as to why he was angry. M. pulled a rolled newspaper from his pocket, held it out. Cheer up, man, he said, have a gander. It's your lucky day.

Lucky? What was lucky about it, he wondered as he took the paper and sat down to eat his breakfast. M. went to the window, squinted through the peephole. Not much out there, is there? he said. Lucky you, you're for havin' a visitor today.

Lucky me, echoed the Professor as he cracked open his egg, noting that it wasn't as hard as he would've liked.

Someone to help you with your work, said M.

Help? said the Professor. I need no help.

This is a big job, said M.

I'm the only one who understands this, said the Professor.

Sure I know that, said M. But you'll be needing some company. This work is, ah, is, is stressful.

Was there anything wrong with the prototype, said the Professor.

Naw, it was great, they were all great, said M. But this is the big one, we don't want any fuckups. This is too important.

The Professor chewed slowly, thoughtfully. I'm glad you realize that, he said. God doesn't play dice with the universe.

Jasus, said M. You're just the Pope in disguise!

Now M. had an ear to the door, a hand on the nob, as if he thought their conversation was being listened to. Before he left, he said, any more requests? The Professor said, yes, please stop moving me around. For a second M. was puzzled by this, then laughed. If you're not in the same place you were yesterday, M. said, then I'm as crackers as you! The Professor watched M. leave, then looked at the newspaper. The front page was taken up with another atrocity, a huge bomb which had killed a lot of soldiers and civilians. The whole thing had been an ambush, it said. The bomb had been detonated by remote control, it said. Very sophisticated. Several buildings destroyed and the crater the biggest ever seen in the city, etcetera, etcetera. Well, there was nothing new in this, it was always was the same... in fact, had M. tricked him? Was this the same paper he read the last time? He looked at the date... Friday, was this Friday? He didn't know.

News didn't interest him anyway. He went to the Classifieds, polished his reading glasses with the sleeve of his shirt, began scanning the columns of places to rent. *Furnished rooms with studio possibilities... close to the City Hall... non-smoking, Catholic gent preferred...weekly, monthly rates.* Was this him? Was he the lodger they wanted? Or was it a flat... he would prefer a flat. He needed the privacy of a flat to do his work, to construct his Machine. Studio possibilities, it said.

He was copying down the phone number when the woman came into the room. She was quite young, dressed the way girls did these days, tight jeans and a leather jacket, and her hair was too red to be real. Who was she?

The bathroom is free, she said, if you need it. Then, aware that the Professor was suspicious, she added: I'm here in place of Fergus.

Fergus, Fergus. Yes, he could remember Fergus. Fergus was his assistant, the lad who had helped him assemble the Prototype. He must be sick.

Later, when he'd finished cleaning himself up in the bathroom, he came out to find her leaning against the wall, smoking a cigarette. Her eyes flicked over his naked chest and arms. She shook her head slowly, said, they told me you were absent-minded... or was it witless? At first he didn't know what she was going on about, then realized he'd forgotten to put on his shirt. Someone had set out a clean one for him, too, but he'd forgotten; he was too busy inside his head.

No smoking, he said to her, trying to bury his shame. Up yours, she said, but stubbed it when she straightened against the wall to let him past.

He was at the peephole in the window looking at the big yellow gantry. It was like a huge metal God, an effigy for a civilization of robots. He could see the control cabin in the superstructure, although he couldn't see if anyone was in there. The machine was still, inactive, religious. Suddenly there were three white flashes in the cabin, as if someone was communicating in semaphore. What was it? The sun on the glass?

What's that, he said. The woman, who was reclining on the bed, looked up from the newspaper, said, aren't you supposed to be working? But he remained at the peephole, hoping to see another flash. What's that machine, he said. The shipyard, she said. You know that.

Of course, of course, he said. They're trying to signal.

She jumped up and scrambled to the window, pushed him aside roughly. She placed her hands on the frame and leaned into the peephole. He went back to his desk, pretended to study the diagram in his notebook, but his eyes wandered back to woman, now aware that she was a shapely young creature, despite the fake trimmings. I see sweet bugger all, she said. What sort of signal are you talking about? A flash, he said. Is that all, she said. Just a reflection... there's a hole in the clouds....

She was standing behind him, over him. You should be going about your work or the both of us will be in trouble, she said. He felt peculiar, conscious of the heat-shadow from her breasts. What's your name, he said. Name, she said bitterly. In our business, what's in a name? You better get to work. Alright, he said, and picked up the soldering iron.

I'd like to go somewhere else, she said. Before it's too late. They say I could go to South America, a sort of a student exchange thing, you know? One of us for one of them. It's not so easy for them to blend in here, the language, the way they look. It's different going the other way, because they're mostly in the jungle or in the mountains. It's not an urban thing, you don't have much contact with the public. They want some of us to get that kind of training. I know some people who went to North Africa, said it was great. Your pal Fergus went there, didn't he? I hear things have cooled between us and them, though, so I'll be going to South America if I'm going anywhere... unless they send me to the mainland again. It's hard on the love life, isn't it?

He said, you're not old enough to be married, are you.

She said, I'm older than I look.

He said, do you have a job?

She said, this is me job, stupid.

He said, you're full-time?

She said, aren't you?

He looked at the circuit board he'd just finished, the symmetry of it, the elegance, the simplicity, all this and déjà vu. One a day, every day the same, all prototypes. He was full-time, alright. He couldn't think of anything else. Even when she told him that Fergus had been killed on the last operation, it had little meaning. He could barely remember him although, obviously, they'd been comrades. He could only think of the machine he was building, and beyond that, this room, the corridor outside, the bathroom at the end, and beyond that, *singularity.*

He said, do you know what it's like to have a conscience, yet have no memory of who or what you are at all?

For the first time, something like pity came into the green eyes of the woman on the bed.

When M. came in with some lunch and found the telephone number on the desk, he shouted in anger, then touched his receding hair in a compulsive, nervous manner with his hand. What the hell was this? Who was the Professor planning to phone? Was he thinking of leaving? The Professor looked at the dry piece of meat on the plate.

It was hard to concentrate on the business at hand. This M. fellow was beneath contempt. Who could eat this except a dog? And if he had the jaws of a dog, he would bite the bastard.

The woman said, no tactical stuff was talked about.

M. said, well how does he know about Fergus?

The woman said, he read it in the paper.

M. said, the paper names no names.

The woman said, you're gettin' on my nerves.

M. said, comrade, remember who you're talking with. Let's step outside and have a wee discussion.

The woman shrugged, but didn't turn around; instead she put her eye to the peephole. She looked out for a moment, then said, what's it like out there? Is it sunny? M. looked at her dumbly. She said, I just saw a flash. M. strode over and took a look, then said, you've been listening to him, haven't you? There's nothing out there, and if there was, we would know....

It begins with a flash, and it ends with a flash, said the Professor. I'm not making a Time Machine. I want to send a message, a message about the meaning of life, the universe, what's going on. Of course it's small, small as a computer a clerk uses in a shop. Size is of little importance, except for style... it's the *mass* that matters. It's a neutron mass... ten to the power of ninety four grams per cubic centimetre, to be exact. The power of this machine will be sensational. Imagine a city, a planet, a galaxy, collapsing on itself... everything, everyone, reduced to an *instant*. Boom — the biggest flash of all.

The woman was combing his hair, finding gray ones, plucking them out. Her job was to pacify him. During their conversation outside the room, M. had made that very clear. There was a big operation coming down and they needed this bomb.

You wouldn't be exaggerating, would you? the woman said.

I believe you know my earlier work, he said.

You're famous, she said. There's a ten thousand pound reward for your arrest.

This was news to him... or was it? Deep down, he knew it was so, for he must've read it in the newspaper or heard it from M. He was a hunted man. He couldn't put a face on the enemy, or put a face on himself for that matter. His amnesia had left him without an identity. He could remember all the mathematics, all the mechanics, all the quantum logic, all the science, and he understood the cosmological focus for his being, but he couldn't remember who he was or why he was.

She parted the hair at the back of his cranium, stopped, said, did you take a bullet here?

The touch of her hands had put him in a trance. All he could manage was, who would want to shoot me?

Just before nightfall M. came in with what he called the "fuel". It was like a large lump of dough, although the Professor thought of it as a brain. With the reverence of a priest, he lifted it slowly and placed it in the cradle between the circuit boards. M. watched with the fascination of a child who has just discovered fear. A nervous tic flickered faintly from his one good eye down his unshaven face. Even the woman was standing in anticipation.

Before I arm this, said the Professor, I want to know two things.

M. looked at the woman, who remained expressionless. M. said, get on with it, man. They're waiting to begin the Op.

Two things, said the Professor. What's your name, and, and why have you moved me again?

M. was baffled, even though he knew the Professor had a memory problem, was used to his ballocks. The woman said, I told him the shipyard thing is on rails and they keep movin' it, so sometimes you see it, sometimes you don't.

M. swore, said, didn't I tell you to stay away from that bloody window? You should keep your mind on your work, not on what might or might not be goin' on out there!

The Professor said, is this true?

M. said, take a look for yourself, then finish your job.

The Professor got up from his desk and went to the peephole. The sky was red above the rooftops. As he looked, the gantry slowly rolled into view, the red hazard lights blinking on its yellow superstructure. It stopped, and then, as if this were a signal, a window in the cabin opened and the barrel of a rifle stuck out. Then, on the flat roofs of the industrial wasteland, armed figures materialized, moving from cover to cover in his direction. M., with the only refined instinct he had, knew immediately something was wrong. He shouldered the Professor aside and leaned into the peephole. When he stepped back, his face was hard, like stone. He said to the woman, they're onto us... you know what to do. Then he ran from the room, not bothering to close the door.

The Professor sat down at his desk and casually made the final adjustment. When he looked up, the woman was taking an automatic pistol from an inside pocket in her leather jacket. With her free hand, she removed her wig and tossed it onto the bed. She was really a blond, and the better looking for it too.

He said, you never told me your name.

She said, you wouldn't remember it anyway.

He said, I knew they were signalling... but you didn't take me seriously.

She was assuming the professional shooting stance, feet apart, weapon clutched in both hands. She said, no, we take you very seriously.

She took aim.

I regret this, she said.

No you won't, he said.

He pressed the trigger on the *Singularity Machine*. In that instant, just as the flash began its acceleration to infinity, his life framed past. It was all there, from beginning to end, and beyond. The university, politics, the murder of his wife, his own escape from death and his partial recovery, his induction into the Organization, the names of his comrades, the faces of his victims... and finally, the future, which he was pleased to share.

The Yank

I.

THE PRISONER SAYS he first went into the plantation with his sister for a picnic, and the trees started talking to him, told him to attack her. He admits that he did attack her sexually, but denies he raped her. This incident occurred two years ago. He says that every time he goes to the plantation, the place makes him feel strange, that the trees put ideas into his head. He admits to raping the Craig girl, yet insists that her cousin was more than willing. This is unlikely. Both girls had their hands tied with industrial tape, although the cousin was able to escape and get help. The Craig girl took a terrible beating, was left tied to a tree, with a star carved into the bark above her head. There were obscenities carved on other trees in the vicinity. During a two hour search of the woods we found the remains of three adult humans. They had been buried in shallow depressions in different spots in or near the thickest grove. The prisoner was found hiding by a wall in the ruins of the old flax mill with the Craig girl's knickers over his head. He was like a zombie. No inducements could get him to talk, even after some heavy RR interrogation. The following day he appeared normal, contrite. He confessed to the Craig rape. He continues to deny any knowledge of the other three victims or of having any hand in their deaths.

II.

"Dr. Ra", a friend of the Organization, has been escorted to the grave sites. His opinion is that the remains are those of young women, and that they were murdered, probably by strangulation. He says the neck vertebra on one of the skeletons is damaged. He says it would take a Lab autopsy to determine just how long they have been there, but he thinks no more than two or three years. A unit is presently searching the plantation to see if there are more bodies. While it is not certain who these women are, we do know that a couple have gone missing in the district in the last while. It was thought that the McLaughlin girl had skipped to the mainland to look for work, for example. We are preparing a further RR session for the Prisoner. In my opinion, the man is guilty, guilty as hell.

As you know, Ireland has no Capital punishment. Turning the Prisoner over to the authorities would be useless, and would certainly lead to him naming names, dates, incidents and the like which could be very harmful to the Organization. His is disloyal and untrustworthy, and to boot, clearly a lunatic. Neither God nor country could defend his actions. I recommend that he be dwarfed.

Alpha

2.

You will have read *Alpha's* report on the Colgin youth, and what is there to say? It is a shocking story all round. He is only eighteen, and while he was an unreliable recruit for us, I would never have guessed he was off his head. Never. An uncontrollable cock is one thing, murder quite another.

He says he didn't kill anyone, and as yet there is no hard evidence to prove he did. It is all circumstantial.

And I must say I am against these Romper Room interrogations on principle. Are we no better than the Provos or the Sandinistas?

I know the woods in question: they are the large plantation on what was once General Black's estate. Black was a hero in the Boer war, you'll recall, and after his death the estate was broken into two farms, the largest of which is still owned by a relative of mine. It is a lonely place, with a very melancholy atmosphere. There is a legend that says it was a Druid shrine, because there are some queer standing stones hidden away in the thickest parts. The lad says the trees talked to him, and the way the wind moves through there, perhaps that's what he thought. Some people talk about banshees, ghosts, that sort of thing. Who is to say?

I'm thinking there's more to this than the supernatural, however. You remember when the Yanks were stationed in this country during the War? They had a barracks in that very plantation. You can still see the odd piece of a foundation for one of their Nissan huts if you take a walk through there. The way *Alpha* describes it, the so-called graves of those young girls might be abandoned trenches. I remember a number of girls went missing in 1944, just before the Yanks pulled out for the European Theatre. There was a lot of talk at the time. Two of them were supposed to have gone up to Belfast for a spree, got killed in a German air raid. This was never proven, and no one ever saw them again, or saw the others who supposedly ran off to England to find work or shack up with one of the Yanks. There was some talk of murder at the time. I know the R.U.C. did some investigating. But as there were no bodies, and the politics were delicate, the investigation evaporated.

And the Yanks left.

Except one. He was Irish to begin with, had emigrated to New York during the Depression. The night before his unit was shipped off to fight in Holland, he deserted. While he looked like a Yank, talked like a Yank, spent like a Yank, he was able to revert into country Irish again, and it was a known fact that he living and working on a farm a few miles away. I actually never met him, but I know he courted my cousin Sally. He had a bad reputation, although I have no details, as I was just a cub then. Sally went to England, or was sent to England. She died in a car crash shortly thereafter, or so her mother would like to have people believe. I know she never went to England. Her brother has told me many times he believes she was murdered by the Yank.

Ireland has never been known to have a sex killer, or what they sometimes call a serial killer, so I have my doubts about the guilt of this young lad Colgin. He might be starkers. He might be. We shouldn't be too hasty here. I think Brother *Alpha* is overly fond of liquidations, regardless of whether or not they will serve the political objective. Colgin has been unreliable, agreed; the truth is, many of our young recruits are. They lack serious commitment, their social life comes first. A bullet through his left hand should be enough of a warning.

Also, I have my doubts about the reliability of our friend "Dr. Ra" when it comes to medical science, and he says himself a proper autopsy is required before one can tell how long those women have been lying in that plantation, never mind who they might be. "Ra" is OK. for stitching up a bullet wound or sharing a glass of the good stuff with, but no good for making this kind of call. The matter is too serious to be solved internally. Therefore I recommend that we let the police have Colgin and let them investigate the matter of these rapes and especially these human remains. Inspector McWhirter owes me one, so the Organization has nothing to fear from any babbling Colgin might do. After all, the young lad is obviously "deranged".

Beta

3.

I value the opinions of Brothers *Alpha* and *Beta*. It is due to the resolve of comrades such as them that Ulster will remain free.

Therefore I have investigated this matter personally. I supervised the last RR interrogation of the Prisoner myself, and am pleased to report that he gave a full confession. Not even God can stand between him and everlasting Hell for the heinous crimes he has committed. His poor young sister and the Craig girls were the lucky ones, for they at least escaped Death. Tragically, there is nothing we can do for the six young women he murdered in the insane expression of his lust. Six, yes. We will find the others. There will be Justice, nevertheless, even if it is a small Justice.

I believe Brother *Beta* has allowed his personal tragedy to divert his eyes from seeing the truth of the situation. His anecdote about Sally and "the Yank" is interesting — even touching, I might add — but what have the events of forty years ago got to do with the reality of modern Ulster? It is true that many of our enemies find safe haven in America. America even gives them money and arms. But we have friends in America too, and they have been generous to the Organization. I have visited America, and can vouch for the fact that they aren't all thieves and killers and Fenian bagmen. And let us not forget the American servicemen who helped defeat Hitler and the Nazi menace. We owe them much for ensuring the survival of the institutions we revere, such as the British Monarchy.

But it is now up to us to be vigilant.

Therefore I have ordered *Alpha* unit to carry out the execution of the Prisoner within 24 hours. Further, I have ordered *Alpha* unit to Sector 6 of American Infantry Camp N.I. 3 where they will collect all human remains for immediate disposal.

It is not necessary to remove any of the trees or their sick *graffiti.* They can serve as a temporary monument to remind any who enter those woods that there can be *No Surrender!* I trust you will understand the urgency in the situation and why I have issued these orders on my own authority.

Omega.

The List

STUDENT "X" WAS FEELING VERY GOOD that day: he'd inherited a boxed set of Glen Miller classics from that fella who'd just just blown his year at Queen's and gone back to Canada, and into the bargain he'd received a good mark on his Anatomy essay, a very good mark indeed. So he ordered the best, a Black Bushmills, and settled down in the corner by himself to have a gander at the Belfast News Letter. Bottom of the front page was an article about the Provos receiving training in Libya...that seemed interesting; for a brief moment he imagined himself in the North African desert drinking mint tea in the cool shade of a date palm as he watched a group of thugs from the Falls Road learning how to transform camel dung into a high-powered explosive. The I.R.A. in Libya — what the hell for? It had to be a public relations act for there was nothing Kadaffi could teach those buggers — didn't they invent the car-bomb in Belfast? They did. Copied the world over. When it came to terrorism, there was nothing you could teach the Irish. Except how to play Swing.

He was just folding the front page back when he realized he was being watched by the man with the black scarf wrapped around his throat at the table by the door. Annoyed, X decided to lock eyes and stare the blirt down... but after a moment he realized the man was in a trance, probably drunk, was questioning the future, not him. Yet when

X returned to his newspaper, the man suddenly stood up, banged against the table, and lunged out of the bar, leaving his empty pint glass wobbling beside the black ashtray. There was only one other patron in the place, an old gaffer who was sitting at the counter talking with the barman. The barman's eyes flicked briefly in the direction of the door, but obviously there was nothing special in this exit for him.

The man left something else other than an empty glass too: a piece of paper on the padded wall bench. Might've dropped from his pocket or perhaps he set it there and forgot it. As X sat there thinking about the incident, his curiosity deepened, until he found himself walking across to the table, picking up the ashtray with one hand, and, using his body as a shield, the piece of paper with the other. He didn't smoke but he had a piece of gum and when he returned to his corner, he took it from his mouth and dropped it into the ashtray. There was only one butt, and it had lipstick on it. Perhaps Black Scarf had been with a woman before X came in. Perhaps they'd had a tiff and now Black Scarf was out hunting the streets for her.

He unfolded the piece of paper; it was a list of names, with professionally typed short biographies. What was it? A salesman's list of prospective clients? There was something odd about the bio's, because not only did they give the usual data about age, home address, and occupation, they also had a few lines about how these people travelled to work and when. This one, for instance: *John McCloskey, 23, of 1916 Chambers Street, apprentice electrician with DeLorean. Bicycle. Leaves home at 7.05 am, leaves work at 4.25. Sometimes works shift. Pubs: The Rotterdam, The Sacred Heart, Kelly's....* Well, the man was obviously a Catholic. And so was this one: *Harold Connors, 19, of 308 North Circuit Road, unemployed labourer, last with Babcock-Wilcox. Drives a green Commer van, RUR069. Pubs: Kelly's, American Giggilo, Ferry Boat Inn, The Dundalk.* There were seven names in all, and two of them were women. He recognized the last one.

It was Kerry, Kerry Monaghan, and X didn't need to read the piece of paper to know she was 20 and a student at

Queen's and that sometimes she drove her father's red Mini Cooper and that her favourite pubs were the Botanic and this one. He didn't know her that well, mind you, although he'd faced her once... when was that? More than a year ago up in Portrush, when he'd picked her up at a dance in the Arcadia Ballroom and walked her back to her hotel. Her front teeth were gold plated and clinked against his when they kissed. Back in Belfast, she gave him the freeze, acted as if nothing had ever happened. It was the oddest thing, because she danced so well, knew all the old ones like the Quick Step and The Fox Trot, and liked the old dance band music and he thought they were in love, just like that, in love, first time around.

But it was one of those weekend romances, an easy fantasy for a couple of evenings in a resort town, and then, back in the real world, in Belfast, you stayed with your own kind. He'd seen her a number of times around the university, but she'd always ignored him. It wasn't just politics, it was a class thing, for she was from a merchant family, and her denial made him angry. They could at least be civil to one another, couldn't they? Considering the fact that he'd had his tongue in her mouth, you'd think she could smile and be polite.

The bar was beginning to fill up with the lunch-time crowd, mostly students, but as he had a second whiskey and pondered the meaning of this very odd list, he was hardly aware of them. On the back of the page was a diagram, a pyramid made up of two triangles on the bottom supporting one on top. At each corner of each triangle were the initials of someone on the list. It was like a map of a secret society, or... his heart began to thud as he looked up and saw Kerry Monaghan come in and sit down in almost exactly the same spot that Black Scarf had occupied earlier. She was carrying a large shopping bag which she pushed below the table with her feet. There were three other girls at the table and soon Kerry was laughing and smoking along with them, and although she must've seen him by now, she avoided eye contact. His heart was hammering so madly he thought the drink had gone to his head; his face was hot and he felt wet with sweat below his shirt.

He went into the The Gents and flushed the list down the toilet, all the while thinking Black Scarf would come in and shoot him. He was a hard-looking egg, no doubt about it. A teeth-grinder. Not that X was a weakling himself, he could lift his own weight and more and throw it, but there were no fair fights any more. All you had to do was read the graffiti: *Abortions For The Papists! Divorce For The Dogan!*

Back in his corner he thought, well, I'll have to tell her. I'll have to tell she's marked. There's man out there with a Black Scarf waiting for you. But the longer he sat there, the greater the funk he got into and then some people came in and wanted his table, so he had no choice but to share or leave. It was ridiculous but he felt the whole bar was watching him. He passed his hand through his hair and started towards her. She was showing her friends a green cardigan she'd taken from her shopping bag, and when he came to their table, he had to linger like a servile waiter before he could get her attention. Her friends stopped their chatter and their eyes scaled him swiftly, and then they looked expectantly at their friend. Kerry finished folding the cardigan, then turned and looked at him. She had no lipstick on, and her gold teeth were hidden inside a closed, disciplined mouth. Kerry, he said. That was all. The words had failed him, and he was forced to turn away, head down, and push through the door to the gray outside, the list hidden in his mind like the dance they once had together in a time when things were different.

A Small Legacy

JAMES THOMPSON, EX-PATRIATE... or how about, James
Thompson, Exile? He scribbled both versions on the back
of his old Glasgow-Belfast steamship ticket, then tried James
Thompson, R.I.P. It was no good either. All three signatures
had the false promise of a cheque from a member of the
lesser nobility, something to fool a barman or an obsequi-
ous tailor. Jesus, he was 21 and he still hadn't settled on a
signature. He was nothing. He had no career, no vocation,
and he wasn't even sure he had a country.

What was he doing here in Joe's Cafe for that matter? Fake
Hollywood decor and memories of chips and beans, pow-
der and perfume, and the tactless jokes of those who used
to be his friends. Yes, friends and lovers, enemies and family, where were they now? His hand crossed his stubbled
face until his fingers found his throat and checked his
glands. He hadn't shaved for two weeks, the two weeks
since the funeral. He still felt ill.

The door bell chimed and he saw Duck enter and come
towards him as if it were a regular Saturday night and they
were going to head down the Balmoral Road and see if they
could pick up some women for a feel in the bushes. Mind
you, Duck had never been a friend, a real pal, but he was a
contemporary. He knew a lot about women. James could
talk to him. Duck would understand.

Duck didn't even bother to remove his rain coat or sit

down. He said, long time no see, you still at the Tech? James shook his head, rotated his coffee mug in his damp hands. Duck smiled faintly and James could see that he still hadn't bothered to get his teeth fixed. They were dirty, like his jokes, his approach to life. Or perhaps he had changed. James had changed: he now combed his hair a different way, like a monk, because he felt like a monk.

Duck didn't seem to notice. He leaned over the table, said, I need to talk to someone, I'm in a bind, want to go for a drink, a real drink? They locked eyes for a moment, then James got up and followed Duck through the nearly deserted Cafe. Outside, it was still overcast and the pavement was patchy from the last shower. As they walked down the street and Duck talked about university and Belfast, James realized that Duck was completely unaware that he had been away for nearly three years, in Canada for two, England and Scotland for another, nearly been married, nearly been dead, was with the dead, yes, with the dead even now as he and Duck walked past their old school, intimate as brothers.

They ended up in the lounge of the Adair Arms Hotel, the most expensive place in town. Duck had a Guinness, while James had a Carlsberg lager. On the second round, at James's suggestion, Duck added a brandy as a chaser. Still, for all this and Duck's natural lack of inhibition, James couldn't believe the frivolous nature of his acquaintance's story. I'm doing my *practicum* in this school in north Belfast, said Duck, and she comes into clean the classroom when I'm there marking lessons. She's just an awful woman, a bloody skivvy, but I've got to have her, you understand? Just got to... but I'm damned if I know how to go about it. To James, this was absurd. A parade of female faces floated before him, victims of Duck's relentless pursuit, girls from the dances and the shadows of the Balmoral Road, women from the streets of Belfast, women from the ditches of his dreams. I don't understand, said James, his eyes glazed, comprehending Duck in the near past, here now as a ghost or an imposter. I don't understand it either, said Duck. He stubbed out his cigarette, lit another. Well I do, actually. Me way's not clear, I can't move on her because Nan's pregnant...

I've been going with Nan for two years. You wouldn't know her. She's in the same year as me at Stranmillis. Christ, James, it's a terrible bind I'm in, terrible, damned if I know what I can do.

Two years, said James. A long time.

Too long, said Duck. How am I going to get rid of her?

I nearly got married, said James.

How'd you get rid of her?

My grandmother died. The woman who reared me. So I just up and left... I was in Canada, so I had to come back.

For the first time, Duck looked at James as if he were important, as if James's experience just might match his own. But he didn't say: What were you doing in Canada? or England or Scotland or even: What are you doing here? No. Duck said, tell me how you got rid of her... this woman you nearly married.

James could feel the alcohol working on him; he hadn't eaten properly in days. There were three business men nearby with a laughing secretary, and a couple of cattle dealers standing at the bar, their sticks hooked on their left forearms. All of them seemed familiar, as if they were relatives, or the friends of relatives. He helped himself to one of Duck's cigarettes before starting. I had a dream, he said. I dreamt that my granny was dying. I could see her lying in this bedroom we hardly ever use, the one with the view of Slemish, and she was dying. It's the room where everyone in our family dies. One of her sons, my Uncle Alex who I never knew, died there and that's where I saw my grandfather in his coffin. The dream was very vivid, and it made me wake up, and when I went downstairs there was a telegram for me saying my grandmother was very ill and not expected to live.

Duck nodded slowly, said, that's a perfect excuse.

James said, no it isn't. I loved my fiance. I didn't want to leave her.

Absolutely perfect, Thompson. Christ I would use it myself if I could, but Nan would never swallow it. I need money. She knows where she can get an abortion.... Duck's expression became gloomy as he stared into the dregs of his Guinness. I just don't have the cash, he said, and I'm certainly in no position to pay her to have it.

A perfect excuse. At this moment Duck's callous, self-interested statement brought James to a moment of truth: *he had used his grandmother's death as an excuse to break the engagement.* So it was a double-death he was experiencing, one sexual, the other maternal. As he tried to imagine his fiance, her face was obliterated by the gaping, toothless hole of his grandmother's death gasp.

What could he do? Where could he go?

He realized he'd written his name on the back of his coaster: *James Thompson.* This time, it looked important, like the signature of an artist. He said to Duck, how much do you need for this abortion? Duck shrugged, said, fifty quid. James said, if I give you thirty, can you get the rest? Duck nodded, said, did your granny leave you some money? Yes, said James. Not much. A small legacy. Do you have the money on you, said Duck. I can write a cheque, said James. You've got thirty minutes to walk up to my bank. The Northern.

He wrote out the cheque and as Duck admired the signature, he realized he was twisted so badly he didn't know who or what to hate: some women, all women, or Life. In the meantime he hated himself. He hadn't been aware of the true extent of this self-hatred until this moment as he stood and shook hands with Duck, saying, good luck with the skivvy, mate. He watched him leave, Duck moving swiftly through the lounge, eager not to miss the Bank or his destiny. Jesus, he looked like a gimp in that raincoat, some old blirt you'd see shuffling up the Cliftonville Road looking for a stray greyhound. James raised his hand and ordered another drink. Why not? He could afford it, he had a small legacy, one he didn't really need. After all, he was free, wasn't he?

The Garden

WHERE WAS HIS mummy? His daddy, he thought, was dead. But his mummy had brought him here and left him in the garden, said she would be back just as soon as she put the key back on the hook in the pantry. Where was she? She'd been gone a long time.

He looked up at the wall. It was high, bigger than his grandpa's horse, so high all he could see were clouds and blue pools. He stood up and looked expectantly towards the red door in the wall. It was still closed. Well, he would walk. He would walk the path that followed the wall.

They went on forever, the path and the wall, although they were turning to the left, so perhaps they were arriving somewhere. It was a long way, though, and the garden was very big. There were apple trees, blackcurrant bushes, and other prickly bushes where the stinging bees liked to hide. He was walking faster now, and soon he was running, even though the path was becoming lost in rough grass and wild ivy.

He stumbled, then fell. He lay there panting, drawing in the scented air as if he was drinking milk after playing. What was that? Was someone calling? He held his breath; all he could hear was the thumping of his heart. It was thumping just like the wheels of the train on the railways tracks that brought him here. Is this where I'm going to live, he wondered. Or is it just a holiday as his mummy said it was. His mother: the most beautiful woman in the world.

He listened: but now a silence fell back at him from the mysterious sky with its castles and its pools. The silence covered him like snow. He was numb. He tried to rise up and run back the way he'd come, but he couldn't move because of this new thing, this fear that was in him like the wall that curves forever.

II.

How long had he been here? Too damned long. This was no place for a fella with places to go, movies to see, girls to meet. He was the only one working in the garden that day. It was his responsibility to fill those three buckets with blackcurrants. He'd laboured all day in the beating sun to fill two of them when a sudden shower forced him to take shelter in the potting shed. The walls were crumbling and red ivy tore at the dry masonry and rafters like silent flames. Stacks of neglected clay pots and abandoned wooden flats littered the place; none of them had ever been used as long as he could remember. The garden was going to ruin and the occasional harvesting of the berries was about all the place was good for. It was old, like stones, old, like his grandmother.

He examined his hands: they were red from stripping the berries from their branches. Briefly, he considered masturbation. Then someone was calling him; it was distant, like a wave rising and falling against the garden wall. He listened impersonally until the caller gave up, and he was left with the solitude of the lessening rain.

Yet his mind could move from rain to sunshine with the eagerness of youth. He shifted position so that the cobwebs no longer obscured his view of the lawn, the large rectangle of grass that he'd personally restored. The shower had brought out the stripes left by the mower, which sat nearby exuding the comforting smell of oil. He went over and gripped the wooden handles, opened the silver throttle with his thumb, imagining the vibration of the engine in the steel shafts. It was a thing of beauty, the mower. The spiralled blades, the heavy roller, the chain that moved them — there was a cause and effect here that he could admire. Cutting grass was more interesting than picking fruit... but it was his responsibility to do both.

He felt hungry and decided to head for the house. The rain had passed now, leaving the sagging bushes wet and glistening, difficult to work in. He crossed the lawn, jumped a low hedge, then came to the red door. But it was locked, locked from the outside — someone had locked him in! He cursed, looked up at the wall; it was twice his height but not impossible. There were trees he could use to help himself up, although, once up, the drop to the outside was something else again. There would be nothing to break his fall but the unsympathetic stones.

He looked at the door, the wall, the breaking sky above. He thought about his responsibility, and the absurdity of his situation.

He started walking along the path slowly. He was thinking about movies, girls, music on the radio. Then he saw the two full buckets of currants that he'd forgotten to cover in his hurry to get out of the rain: a large white bird was perched on one, gorging itself with the fruit of the other. It was the largest bird he'd ever seen, big as a swan or bigger. He stood transfixed until the bird had finished, then watched as it extended its huge wings and flew effortlessly from the garden.

III.

He was old now, but not old enough to stay in bed all day. He could see the garden. He wasn't looking through the window or at a photograph. It was trapped inside of him as if his skull were a stone helmet.

Only the wall with its rude geometry made sense — the rest was a jungle. The avenues with their low Renaissance hedges and Italianate mapping were gone, displaced by a somber chorus of coarse grass, weeds, ivy, wild bushes. The fruit trees were now barren, webbed together like kneeling skeletons. Soon they would be mere sediment.

He thought he had escaped. He'd gone to another country, changed his identity. He did this by neglecting his memories so that, at best, they were not memories but dreams founded in nothing personal. They might come from books or movies or from someone's conversation, but they didn't come from him. The past was all imaginary.

But then, are not all emotions linked by a common avenue? When he was sad, it was inevitable that he would think of the garden, and while he could always dismiss it as something imaginary, the garden would be there, and now that he was sad all of the time, the garden was as real as the wound on his head. He'd fallen on the steps when he paused to watch the gulls landing on the blue waters below his property. He'd hurt his back too and his back had been bad any-way.

He was kneeling by the couch where he'd dropped the remote control, wondering how he could get back up without falling over. The television was silent, the house too, but he could hear the water lapping as a fisherman passed. Whatever way he moved, there would be pain, so he remained kneeling, angry and sad that he was too fragile to fight. In his helplessness he remembered his young mother sleeping in bed, his father in the sky. He was in the garden again, not as it used to be, but as it was now. The ruin was complete, and only the encircling wall seemed intact. Was someone calling? As he strained to hear, all his senses became focused, his muscles hard, and he was ready to fly....

But in reality, the remote dropped from his hand as he collapsed and folded onto the floor. Who would come? In the beginning, he wanted to be found; later, he wanted to hide; now, he just wanted someone to turn on the television.

Heifer

IS THERE ANYTHING MORE DREARY than a rainy day in Co. Antrim when you're standing in a cattle pen minding the heifers as they swish their tails, maw, rub their flanks on the wall, the railings, each other, maw, swish, shit, shit spilling, splattering, spluttering, shit always on your rubber boots and the flies, and you're looking at the leaden skies and wondering when in God's name these animals will get their turn in the auction and you will be out of there? I think not. I think: *this is why I will never be a farmer, this is why I will stay in school, this is how I will get out of here, away from all this... shit.*

Beyond the wall is the school and I hate that place too, but at least it is clean. Slowly, one group at a time, the farmers move their cattle through the auction, and finally our turn comes and we surrender our heifers to the professional herders who whistle, yelp, and whack the indolent beasts into the holding pens behind the ring. I get rid of my stick immediately, hurling it like a spear of freedom over the wall and head for the tap to wash my Wellingtons, kick the matted dung from the soles, eliminate the sight and smell of shit. But it's everywhere, fresh claps around the cattle lorries and dried ones spotting the sloping gravel grounds of the Fair Yard. The sweating heat, the smell, the close air send me across the yard to buy a bag of potato crisps and a carbonated drink at the small confectioners, although the cattle drovers drink from the tap regardless of the flies. Some farmers are already in the public houses, exchanging luck pennies, spending profits, lamenting losses, but meanwhile the auction continues, and as I walk back through the warm drizzle, I can hear the caller's speeding chant, *whatamIbid whatamIbid whatamIbid* and think, he has the best job of us all.

I enter the auction ring, hear the rain on the corrugated roof as I take a seat in the top row, high above the ring, see my Uncle standing against the white wall that encircles the ring, his stick hooked his arm as he taps a fresh cigarette against the packet, then offers one to some worthy who is leaning beside him. The heifers enter one at a time, trot in dumb confusion around the straw, occasionally struck by the stick of the ringmaster in the dirty white lab coat, his red face boozed to an unhealthy glow. The auctioneer, stationed on his elevated podium, rambles on, *a pound a pound a pound* and none of it makes any sense to me, how long do you have to go to school to understand this bastard? The buyers, sitting here and there, nod, make coded movements, the auctioneer pauses, looks at my uncle who nods, and another heifer is heading for the slaughter house across the water. I'm thinking as I watch them, the white ones, the red ones, the black ones, the piebalds and the zebras, watch them parade the ring, I'm thinking boy a matinee at the *State* would go nicely now, a Western or a Brando flick, even the Three Stooges, anything rather than this. But my dreams are dashed by the red heifer nobody wants even though the buyer in the black suit and black pork-pie hat keeps stepping into the ring and feeling her haunches, groping between her legs, and it might be he has detected something about this featureless creature that I can't see, she looks the same as the others, big as a bullock and just as noisy, but no thanks, the price isn't right, my Uncle shakes his head, and the heifer is driven from the ring. My Uncle turns and looks up, sees me glumly watching, motions me to join him, and I know that this Saturday I will never escape the shit.

I am given the task of herding this animal home. There is no lorry available, apparently, and certainly I am less expensive. He slips a pound note into my hand, and that makes the five miles we must travel seem like one mile and thus, in a rejuvenated frame of mind, I follow the auctioneer's assistant to the reject pen where the red heifer is transferred to my capable custody. I have no stick, but I can clap my hands, stamp my feet, whistle, growl and holler. Soon the heifer is trotting down Mill Street past the parked cars and reclining bicycles, the low walls and privet hedges, the curtained windows of the citizens, and I'm running clumsily to keep up. The first junction is at the Chapel, four roads to the four corners of Ireland, and if I can't get the heifer to enter the right one, I'm doomed. The lack of a stick is a terrible handicap and I'll have no chance of getting another until we are out in the country. Thanks to God and the priest the gate into the Chapel is closed; the idea of the heifer amuck among the gravestones of the Catholic dead is embarrassing, but likewise the possibility of a wrecked garden of the wealthy on the road we must take. Fortunately a passing citizen prevents the heifer from following the roundabout and re-entering the town, and I see it gallop ahead below the chestnut trees and hedges of the rich. Me, I'm walking now, let the bugger run, I feel blisters on my feet, and the humid drizzle is making me smell like a sheep. Also, there's a girl I fancy living somewhere on this suburban road, and I'm mortified at the prospect of being connected to this lowly profession, the country clod covered in shit, running like a graceless yahoo after a stupid red heifer.

All goes well, however. Just where the last house gives way to the fields of the country, I find my heifer standing eating a bush, lustily pulling the leaves into its rolling mouth, and there's no sign of she who makes my heart run fast, my hands stay in my pockets, my face go red, my tongue say silly things, and from here it looks like a leisurely coast to the farm. The traffic is light, the rain has abated, the heifer is inclined to be reasonable. It's beyond me why no one would want her. Her eyes look healthy, her ribs don't show, her belly doesn't sway, and for now, at least, there's no shitting. I am tired, though, and the thought occurs to me to climb on her back, make her work, but I'm knowledge-able enough to know better: you can't milk a bullock, and you can't ride a heifer.

We are within a mile of home when I lose her. I'm asleep on my feet, of course, walking along, dreaming of Rosemary, dreaming of Brando, dreaming of how many ice creams a pound can buy, when she bolts through an open slap in a field near the manse and there she goes heading across the potato drills for the river. The river! Ah, how I would love to idle by the river, bathe my aching feet, listen to the wa-ter falling over the stones, listen to the wind in the trees, just wank off and do nothing, but aw naw, this bloody heifer has me running, and have you ever tried running over a wet potato field, the drills as deep as ditches, and you no strength left at all? I get her cornered and ready to drive back to the road, when damnit to hell's blazes, she bolts down into the river, starts running up the shallows, and I have to follow, break through hedges, get my face and hands tore, keep running and the pain in my heart is kill-ing, Jesus, is this life or is it death or the thing they call both? That heifer has a hole in its left ear and right now I am fit to punch its twin if I can catch her, bloody beast of the devil that she is, splashing up the river, Jesus, disappearing, Je-sus.

An hour or two later, just as dusk comes on, I find her grazing with a herd in another farmer's field. How peace-ful, how serene, how typically mid-Antrim. I have a new stick, freshly torn from the hedge, and I'm itching to use it. But how do I recognize her now that I'm not in my right mind? Not by the hole in her ear, no sir. Not by putting my hand between her haunches, no sir. It's when she lifts her tail and I'm too exhausted to get away in time, that's how.

Well I might be no use for farming and that's a fact, and I might be wet behind the ears, fit only for the company of women taking tea, but I know this: it's a wise man who goes to the Fair with his stick, and it's a fool who returns home without one.

Something Special

ROBINSON WASN'T ON AN ISLAND like Robert Louis
Stevenson or in the desert like D.H. Lawrence or even in a
Paris apartment like Samuel Beckett — whom he'd kicked a
few back with in his day, both of them Irish together and
desperate — but like them he was in exile and would die
that way. Now that he was on the way out, could barely
think coherently any more, he knew at least he'd been suc-
cessful, more than modestly so, his stories were famous and
he'd already joined the pantheon of the great ones.

He was in his bed, in his house, and through the window he could see the snow stretching for miles, a vast ice-
field that revealed the curvature of the earth, and the sense
of something, like a blank piece of paper waiting for the
first sentence. He could see it gleaming in the sunlight, even
though his eyes were closing, and dreams sometimes inter-
fered. His daughter came into the room, fixed his pillow,
straightened the covers, moved delicately trying not to dis-
turb him, assuming he was asleep. She was with him almost
constantly now, his last love, a young woman and soon
married. She was being very brave and capable, very Irish
although she had never been in Ireland, never seen the
greenness of it, the black stones and history always coming at you out of the mist. She had never seen it but perhaps one day she would. She loved the snow, never thought

of it as being anything but the way the world was, even when they travelled in the tropics. This was home for her and it was for him now, although he wondered, especially when his eyes closed.

He could feel her hand on his, and they were like that for a long time, despite the fact that it seemed like no time at all. He became aware of her voice, softly, cool like his mother's, or her mother's, he wasn't sure which, but softly and important: *Daddy... remember the time I was going to run away because you were mean to me and I had my suitcase packed and everything... and you told me the story about how you'd run away when you were little boy in Ireland I think it was and you always travelled in a circle so you would be back in time for dinner... do you remember that Daddy... so I did the same thing and every time I wanted something special I'd run away... remember?*

Something special. Yes, he certainly remembered, but in the remembering he became uneasy. Why? What was wrong with running away? It was years ago, his running away, so long he'd forgotten it and there was something deep and mysterious in the story, especially as his daughter told it, especially as he was hearing it now, and when he thought of all the great stories he'd written in his life, he couldn't understand how he had missed this one. Her hand felt cold, remote, as distant as the horizon beyond the window, and the effort of raising himself up, of waking again, was beyond him. And with infinite sadness he recognized that he had forgotten all the great stories of his life, had repeated the wrong ones entirely, and would never achieve the greatness he thought was his.

Lawrence Russell was born and raised in rural northern Ireland. He came to Canada when he was sixteen. His drama has been performed across Canada and the U.S. He teaches Writing and Film at the University of Victoria, B.C.